Justin D'Ath grew up on a farm in New Zealand, and he wrote his first book (a ten-page cartoon about his pet turtle, Bubble) when he was nine years old. Since then, Justin has had lots of jobs but has never stopped writing. He now lives in Bendigo and is a full-time author, although he still finds time to teach novel writing to adults and run writing workshops with children in schools.

Justin D'Ath's junior novels are inventive and highly entertaining, full of twisted science, unexpected plots and playful use of language.

www.justindath.com

Other books by Justin D'Ath:

Why did the Chykkan Cross the Galaxy?
Sniwt
The Upside-down Girl
Koala Fever
Echidna Mania

For older readers:

Hunters and Warriors

Justin D'Ath

ASTRID SPARK, Fixologist

The girl with the incredible magnetic fingers

Pictures by Terry Denton

ALLEN&UNWIN

First published in 2002

Allen & Unwin
83 Alexander St
Crows Nest NSW 2065
Australia
Phone: (61 2) 8425 0100
Fax: (61 2) 9906 2218
Email: info@allenandunwin.com
Web: www.allenandunwin.com

National Library of Australia
Cataloguing-in-Publication entry:

D'Ath, Justin.
  Astrid Spark, fixologist.

  For children aged 8–12 years.
  ISBN 1 86508 718 1.

  1. Ballooning – Juvenile fiction. I. Denton, Terry, 1950– . II. Title.
A823.3

Cover and text design by Sandra Nobes
Set in 11 pt Veljovic by Tou-Can Design
Printed in Australia by McPherson's Printing Group

10 9 8 7 6 5 4 3

For Rosie

1. Kiss my butterfly

Two eleven-year-old girls stand on the deck of a ship somewhere in the Southern Ocean.

'Astrid,' says one of them, 'you know how we've been best friends ever since we started school?'

'Yes,' says her best friend.

'And you know how best friends do favours for each other?'

'Yes,' says her best friend.

'And how sometimes they even do each other really *special* favours?'

'Yes,' says her best friend.

'Well, Astrid Spark, my very bestest friend in the whole wide world, I've got a really really really *HUGE* favour to ask of you.'

'Yes,' says her very bestest friend in the whole wide world (whose name, in case you haven't noticed, is Astrid Spark).

The first girl's face turns red. 'This is really embarrassing . . .'

'Just say it, Kia-Jane!'

'Astrid, would you please please please please *please* kiss my but– [1]'

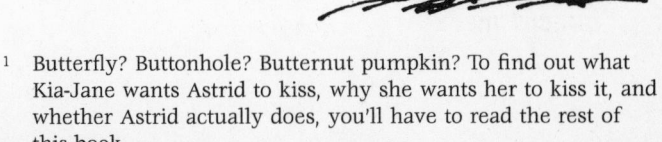

---

[1] Butterfly? Buttonhole? Butternut pumpkin? To find out what Kia-Jane wants Astrid to kiss, why she wants her to kiss it, and whether Astrid actually does, you'll have to read the rest of this book.

2. Four years earlier

What I Did in the Holidays
by Astrid Spark (8 next birthday)

In the holidays my family went to Queensland.
My friend Kia-Jane came too. We went to Ocean
World. A boy teased the orca whale and made it
really mad. It bumped the big window where you
looked through and cracks came in the glass.
Everyone got scared and ran away.

Except me.

I was worried about the orca. If the window
broke, all the water would swish out and none
would be left for the orca to swim in. So I fixed
the glass and the orca was safe.

Next day we visited the Museum. It was the
Ming Pottery Exhibition. An old man accidentally
fainted and broke one of the pretty vases. It cost
one million dollars. They brought a chair for the
old man to sit on. He looked sad. It was because
he had to pay one million dollars for a new vase.
So I fixed the old one and he didn't have to.

At the end of the holidays we flew home. Our
plane went through a thunderstorm. Suddenly
lightning struck. *BOOM!* A long zig-zaggy line came
in the wall of the plane. It was getting bigger.
Lots of people started screaming. Kia-Jane was
the loudest. Everyone thought we would crash.

Except me.

I fixed the wall and everything was okay.

When we arrived home, Mum and Dad said, 'No more adventures, please!'

Kia-Jane and my big brother Felix said it was the coolest holiday ever.

The End

'Astrid Spark!' the Grade 2 teacher called out.

A skinny girl with a small, heart-shaped face and frizzy blond hair looked up. 'Yes, Mr Mantelli?'

'Do you know the difference between fact and fiction?'

She nodded. 'Fact is real, fiction is made up.'

Mr Mantelli handed back her English workbook. 'Next time I ask you to write about what you did in the holidays, Astrid, I want you to write fact, not fiction.'

'But I did write facts, Mr Mantelli.'

'Don't make me laugh!' he said. But it was too late – he *was* laughing, and it caused his glasses to slip off the end of his nose.

They landed on Astrid's desk and broke in two.

'Oh, no!' Mr Mantelli groaned. 'That's my only pair.'

Astrid picked up the two halves of Mr Mantelli's broken glasses and calmly joined them together.

'All fixed,' she said, handing them back.

Her teacher couldn't believe his eyes. (So he put his glasses back on.) 'Astrid, how did you do that?'

She shrugged. 'It's pretty complicated, Mr Mantelli. You'll have to ask my mum to explain it.'

3. Five <u>more</u> years earlier (or, 3 next birthday)

Alien in the family[2]
by Felix Spark (Astrid's big brother)

One day when Astrid was two, Mum dropped a loaf of bread in the hallway while she was bringing in the groceries. It was a sliced loaf. The bag slipped open and bread went everywhere. Mum didn't have time to pick it up because at that very moment the phone started ringing in the next room.

When Mum finished the call and went to pick up the bread, she discovered Astrid had beaten her to it. Not only had Astrid put all the slices tidily back into the bag, she had joined them together. It was a perfect, *unsliced* loaf!

Mum is an astrophysicist, she's pretty smart. It wasn't long before she worked out what had happened.

'Your sister is a fixologist,' Mum told me after school.

'A fixologist?' I said. 'I've never heard of that.'

'Neither had I,' admitted Mum. 'Astrid is the very first one.'

---

[2] An extract from *Echidna Mania*, available at a bookshop near you.

'Is it sort of like being an alien?' It would be so cool having an alien in the family.

'No. It's a person who repairs broken molecular bonds.'

'Oh, I se-e-e-e-e-e-e-e!' I said, nodding and trying to look intelligent.

Mum knew I didn't get it. 'Bread,' she started to explain, 'is made up of tiny particles called – '

'Crumbs.'

'Molecules,' Mum corrected me. 'Molecules are much, much smaller than crumbs. There would be a million of them in a *single* crumb. Astrid is somehow able to join bread molecules back together.'

'But that's crazy!' I said. 'If there are a million molecules in one crumb, it would take Astrid years to join a whole slice.'

'She doesn't do them one at a time, she does them billions at a time.'

'So she's magic!' That would be *better* than an alien.

Mum shook her head. 'Not magic, magnetic.'

Then she explained how molecules are held together by inter-molecular forces, sort of like tiny magnets. It was very complicated. I didn't understand much, except that Astrid had some kind of electricity in her fingers that repaired the inter-molecular forces between bread slices and stuck them back together.

Soon she wasn't just joining bread, she was fixing other things too. Cracked cups. Broken toys.

Dad's Harley Davidson when it fell through a cave in our back lawn.

In fact, there was nothing that Astrid Spark, fixologist, could *not* join back together. Until...

4. Nine years later
(or, 12 next birthday)

The doorbell rang. There was a special extension that ran straight to Astrid's bedroom. She heaved a big sigh and hit the 'pause' button on her CD player.

'Won't your mum answer it?' asked Kia-Jane, who had come over to listen to Astrid's brother's band's new album.[3]

'It'll be for me,' Astrid said wearily.

The two girls traipsed downstairs. A man stood at the front door holding a white cardboard box. Astrid lifted the flap. The box was full of jagged pieces of crystal.

'What was it?'

'A punch bowl,' the man said sadly. He showed

---

[3] Felix was 21 now and part of a very successful band called Echidna.

them a photo. 'That's what it looked like before our daughter's cat knocked it off the sideboard.'

The girls took the carton through to the kitchen and sat down at the table. Using the photo as a guide, Astrid quickly set to work.

'There you go,' she said five minutes later, handing the man his reassembled punch bowl. It looked brand new. 'That'll be twenty dollars, thanks.'

'Astrid!' her mother's voice came from inside.

Astrid gave the man her sweetest, most innocent smile. 'Just kidding. There's no charge.'

'It sucks,' she said to Kia-Jane back in her room. 'Mum and Dad say being a fixologist is a gift, and I'm not allowed to accept money for fixing things.'

'You accept money at school.'

Astrid put a finger to her lips. 'Sssssssh! Not so loud. Mum's ears are like radar.'

'You want to know something?' Kia-Jane whispered. 'I'd *pay* to have a gift like yours.'

'You would not.' Astrid turned the music back on. 'After a week, you'd be sick of it. "Astrid, fix this!", "Astrid, fix that!" I never get a moment's peace.'

The doorbell rang again. This time it was an elderly woman who had broken her false teeth. Astrid hated doing false teeth.

'I don't think they were even washed,' she said to Kia-Jane afterwards.

'Yick!' said Kia-Jane.

'Last week there was a man with a potty. After I'd fixed it, I noticed my fingers were all brown.'

Kia-Jane looked ill. 'Astrid, that is *so* gross!'

'Tell me about it!' Astrid rolled her eyes.

'And you'd *pay* to be a fixologist?'

'Well, maybe not,' her friend admitted, just as the doorbell rang again.

5. Dr Too, I presume?

The man was wearing a large panama hat and a rather old sports jacket with leather patches on the elbows. He had a small greying moustache and a shy but friendly smile.

'Would either of you young ladies be Astrid Spark, the fixogiser?'

'I am,' Kia-Jane said, before Astrid could open her mouth. She waggled her fingers in the air. 'And it's fix-*ologist*, not fixogiser.'

Astrid tried not to giggle as the visitor shook hands with Kia-Jane.

'So, what would you like me to fix?' Kia-Jane asked, in a brisk, businesslike voice.

The man wasn't carrying anything. Behind him, parked outside the front gate, was a small green car with a huge brown-and-white Saint Bernard dog hanging out the window.

'She isn't allowed to fix animals,' Astrid said.

The man followed her gaze. 'No, no, no, no, there's nothing wrong with Marie Curie,' he said. 'I'm the one who needs assistance.'

'She isn't allowed to fix people, either.'

'No, no, no, no, there's nothing wrong with me.'
The man paused. 'Well, there is, actually – one of
my legs is shorter than the other. Look!' He limped
in a quick, bumpy circle, to show them.[4] 'But that's
not why I'm here.' He turned to Kia-Jane. 'I've come
to ask if you'll assist me with an experiment.'

One mention of 'experiment' and Astrid's mother
(who had radar ears, remember?) came racing to the
door. 'I'm very sorry, sir, but my daughter is not a
guinea pig. Her father and I absolutely *will not* allow
her to take part in any experiments.'

The man stuck out his hand. 'I'm delighted to
meet you, Dr Spark.'

Astrid's mother hesitated. 'Hullo, Mr . . . er?'

'Hu,' said the man.

'Who?'

'Exactly!' he said, breaking into a huge smile.
'And it's Doctor, too.'

'Dr Too?'

'No, Dr Hu.'

Dr Spark's eyes widened. 'Not *the* Dr Hu, from
the CSIRO[5]?'

'The very same,' said *the* Dr Hu.

'Why, it's a wonderful, wonderful pleasure to meet
you!' said Dr Spark, clasping Dr Hu's hand in both of
hers. 'I'm a great admirer of your work, Doctor.'

'Why, thank you, Doctor,' said Dr Hu, clasping
Dr Spark's hands in his. 'And let me just say that I'm
a great admirer of *your* work, Doctor.'

Astrid rolled her eyes at Kia-Jane. 'Excuse me,'

---

4   For more about Dr Hu's short leg, see *The Upside-down Girl*,
   available at a bookshop near you.
5   Commonwealth Scientific and Industrial Research Organisation.

she interrupted the two beaming, hand-shaking scientists, 'but what about *my* work?'

They both looked at her blankly.

'Who are you?' asked Dr Hu.

'*I'm* the reason you're here.'

Dr Hu pointed at Kia-Jane. 'No, Astrid is.'

'I'm Astrid,' said Astrid.

'Well, blow me down!' Dr Hu looked back and forth between the two girls. '*Two* Astrids!'

One of the girls nodded, the other shook her head.

'There's only one,' said the head-shaker.

Dr Hu blinked in confusion.

'She was impersonating me,' the real Astrid explained.

The pretend Astrid clasped Dr Hu's hands in both of hers. 'I'm Kia-Jane McKlintock. And let me just say, Doctor Who, that my grandparents absolutely *loved* your TV show.'

'He isn't *that* Dr Who,' whispered Astrid. 'He's *the* Dr Hu.'

'Huh?' said Kia-Jane.

'Hu,' Astrid corrected her. 'He's a famous scientist from the CSIRO.[6] He wanted you – well, me – to help him with an experiment . . . '

'Sorry,' said Astrid's mother. 'My daughter won't be taking part in any experiments.'

[6]   And from *Koala Fever*, available at a bookshop near you.

6. Astrid Spark, you're amazing!

Astrid's parents were strict. She wasn't allowed to fix things for money. She wasn't allowed to fix animals or humans. She wasn't allowed in newspapers, in magazines, on the radio, or on TV. And she wasn't allowed to take part in any scientific experiments.

'We want her to have a normal childhood,' they said.

But Astrid *wasn't* normal. She was the only fixologist in the world. Everybody wanted her to fix things. Or do tricks. Or they wanted to learn her secret.

'There isn't a secret,' Astrid told them. 'I can fix things, but I don't know *how* I do it. I just touch something, and think fixing thoughts, and it gets joined back together.'

Astrid's mother thought she knew how Astrid fixed things, but when she tried to explain it, people either:

(a) didn't understand a word she said;
(b) became more confused;
(c) didn't understand a word she said *and* become more confused; or
(d) went to sleep.

For as far back as Astrid could remember, there had been a steady stream of mad scientists[7], nutty professors[8], doctors[9], boffins[10] and scary-looking men in dark[11] suits arriving at their front door asking her

---

[7] And sane ones.
[8] And nut-free ones.
[9] And nurses.
[10] And biffins.
[11] Or pale, light-weight polyester (in summer).

to assist them with their research. The response they received was always the same.

'Sorry,' Dr and Mr Spark always said. 'Our daughter won't be taking part in any experiments.'

But there had never been anyone like Dr Hu before.

'Most sensible,' he nodded. 'Yes, most sensible indeed. It's much too nice a day to be locked away inside a dusty, fusty laboratory doing boring old experiments!'

Astrid caught Kia-Jane's eye and they both giggled.

The visitor removed his hat. 'Dr Spark, it's been a very long drive up from Sydilly. May I trouble you for a glass of water?'

'Why, certainly,' she said. 'Do come in, Doctor. Would you prefer a cup of tea?'

'Tea would be lovely. But please don't go to any trouble, Doctor.'

'It isn't any trouble, Doctor. I was about to put the kettle on, anyway.'

'In that case, Doctor, I'd be delighted to join you for a cup of tea.'

'Do you like scones, Doctor? I made some this morning.'

'I absolutely love scones, Doctor.' He hesitated, and sniffed the air. 'They wouldn't be . . . *date* scones, by any chance, Doctor?'

'As a matter of fact, Doctor, they are.'

'Doctor, that's my very favourite type of scone!'

The two scientists disappeared inside, leaving Astrid and Kia-Jane in the doorway.

'Doctor,' Kia-Jane said to Astrid, 'do you think the dog might be thirsty, too?'

Astrid nodded. 'I reckon you might be right, Doctor.'

They walked out to the car and began patting the Saint Bernard's huge, saggy head.

'Hi, Marie Curie,' said Astrid.

'That sure is a weird name for a dog,' Kia-Jane commented.

'She was a famous French physicist,' said a strange, squeaky voice.

Both girls jumped back from the dog.

'It talks!' Kia-Jane whispered.

A boy's head popped up behind Marie Curie. 'She invented radium.'

'Your dog invented radium?' asked Astrid.

'No, Marie Curie did,' rasped the boy. His voice was breaking – one moment it squeaked, the next moment it rasped. 'The real Marie Curie,' he squeaked, 'not the dog,' he rasped.

The boy opened the car door and climbed out behind Marie Curie.[12] He was slightly taller than the two girls, and very gangly. 'Hi, I'm Lukas.'

'Are you Dr Whatsit's son?' asked Kia-Jane.

'Dr *Hu's* son,' squeaked Lukas. He had the crookedest teeth the girls had ever seen. 'Dad said I could come up for a drive. Are you Astrid, the fixologist?'

---

[12] The dog, not the famous French physicist.

'My friends call me Super Glue,' said Kia-Jane, repeating her finger-waggling routine. 'Would you like me to fix your teeth?'

'*Kia-Jane!*' hissed Astrid. The boy's face had turned as red as a rose[13]. 'She isn't Astrid,' she explained, 'I am. Would you like a glass of water? You must be hot.'

'I'm okay,' rasped Lukas. 'Marie Curie could probably do with some, though.'

But Marie Curie had already found water. She was up on her back legs, drinking out of the birdbath.

'Marie, *no!*' squeaked Lukas. Too late. The Saint Bernard's enormous weight sent the birdbath toppling. It hit the driveway with a loud thud and cracked neatly in two.

'Doh!' Lukas groaned (well, rasped, actually). 'Marie Curie, you elephant!'

13 I mean as red as a *red* rose – not a pink one, a yellow one, a white one, or one of those orange-and-red stripey ones.

'She can't help being big,' said Astrid.

'Yeah, but she's so clumsy. Now we'll have to buy you a new birdbath.'

'No, you won't. Hold the bits together, you two.'

Two passes of her fixologist's fingers over the broken concrete, and the birdbath was as good as new.

'Unbelievable!' said Lukas, helping Kia-Jane to stand it back up. He turned around. 'Astrid Spark, you're amazing!'

This time it was Astrid's turn to blush bright red.

7. A very interesting theory

Next day Astrid's parents took her and Kia-Jane to the beach.

'We had a visitor yesterday,' Dr Spark mentioned casually, as she and Richard followed the girls onto the sand.

'Only one?' asked her husband.

'Only one scientist.'

Richard began setting up their large green and yellow beach umbrella. 'When will they get the message, Jacqui? Our daughter isn't going to be a guinea pig for any of their stupid experiments.'

'They aren't all stupid,' Jacqui said, but Richard wasn't listening.

'Astrid!' he called. 'Where's your hat?'

'In the car.'

'Go back and get it.' He tossed her the car keys. 'And fetch Kia-Jane's while you're at it.'

'Awww, Dad!' Astrid complained. 'It's windy. They'll blow off.'

'Not if you use your chinstraps,' her father said. 'And leave your T-shirts on unless you're going in the water.'

'They ought to know better,' he grumbled when the girls had gone. 'Don't they know the danger of skin cancer?'

Jacqui was smearing sunscreen over her arms and shoulders. 'Astrid might be able to do something about it.'

Richard nodded. 'She can cover up.'

'I'm not talking about hats and T-shirts,' Jacqui said. 'I'm talking about the cause of the problem.'

'Well, we all know what that is,' said Richard, pointing up at the sky. 'Ultraviolet rays from the sun. Not even Astrid can do anything about those.'

Jacqui was silent for a few moments. She passed the sunscreen to her husband. 'That scientist who came up from Sydilly yesterday,' she said thoughtfully, 'he had a very interesting theory...'

8. Smog and dog

Astrid hadn't been to Sydilly for nearly a year.

'Can we go to Loony Park?' she asked, gazing out at the brown and grey cityscape parading steadily past the train's windows.

'No,' said Jacqui, sitting beside Richard in the seat facing her. 'We didn't take you out of school for the day to go sightseeing.'

Astrid yawned. They had been on the train for nearly three hours. 'Where exactly *is* Dr Hu's laboratory?'

'Right over on the other side of the city,' said Richard. He looked at the map. 'We change trains at Sydilly Central, then we take the South-Western line all the way to the very last stop. Dr Hu said he'd pick us up.'

'We should have driven.'

Jacqui pointed out the window at the heavy smog that cast its dirty brown shadow across the city. 'There are too many cars here already.'

Her mother was right, Astrid realised. When they left home it had been a crisp, clear, sparkly spring morning. Now the sky was filled with dark, poisonous fumes.

'Is that what made the hole in the ozone layer?'

'It's part of the problem,' her mother said. 'But the main offenders are CFCs and halons.'

Astrid yawned again, and hoped Dr Hu wouldn't expect her to know all about CFCs and halons. She was a fixologist, not a scientist.

When they arrived at Dr Hu's station, nobody was there to meet them. They walked out into the deserted car park.

'We're half an hour late,' Richard said. 'Perhaps he grew tired of waiting.'

Jacqui pulled out her mobile phone and punched in Dr Hu's number. 'Hullo, Doctor... Yes, this is Dr Spark. We're at the station. Are you coming to pick us up?'

A large shadow came creeping across the gravel towards them. *Uh-oh!* thought Astrid. *There's a storm brewing.*

'What do you mean, you're already at the station?' her mother was saying into the phone. 'There's nobody here but us!'

Splat! A fat drop of water landed on Astrid's shoulder.

Splat! Another drop landed on her father's hat.

'Above us?' Jacqui was saying into the phone.

The next drop *splat*-ed wetly on the back of Astrid's neck.

'Marie Curie!' squeaked a strangely familiar voice. 'Stop thinking about food!'

All three of them looked up, and received three direct hits – *Splat! Splat! Splat!* – right in the middle of their foreheads.

Hanging in the sky 30 metres above them was an enormous golden balloon. Suspended below it was a car with three heads poking out of the windows. Two of the heads were human; the third (and largest) was canine – a massive brown-and-white Saint Bernard.

'Yick!' squealed Astrid, wiping her forehead (and neck and shoulder) with a tissue.

It wasn't raining – it was drooling!

9. The Baggoon

Dr Hu landed in the railway car park.

'Good morning, Spark family!' he called cheerily out the driver's (or was it pilot's?) window. 'How do you like my baggoon?'

'Bagoon?' said the Spark family.

'With a double G,' explained the scientist (in case anyone was writing a book about it).[14] 'The second G gives it a bit of extra lift.'

Lukas stepped out of the car and politely opened the doors for the Spark family to climb in. 'All aboard,' he said.

'Are you sure it's safe?' asked Astrid's father, peering up at the baggoon which was billowing and swaying above them in a most alarming manner.

---

[14] Somebody was. It's called *Astrid Spark, Fixologist* – available at a bookshop near you.

'Of course it's safe,' Dr Hu said confidently from the driver's/pilot's seat. 'I made it myself.'

It didn't look like any baggoon that Astrid had ever seen. (She had never seen one, actually.) Now that it was closer she realised it wasn't golden, it was transparent – like a giant plastic bag. In fact, it *was* a plastic bag – that's why it was called a baggoon (well, it explained the first G, anyway). The colour came from what was inside it – some sort of weird browny-yellow gas swirling with millions of golden bubbles.

The car was an old red Holden – a station wagon – with one green door and one blue door.[15] On its roof was a large plastic drum mounted on a complicated arrangement of wheels, levers and springs. It looked a bit like a giant cocktail shaker. A thick rubber hose ran from it up into the baggoon.

Instead of wheels, the Holden had strange, round paddles, and clamped onto the tailgate was an oily outboard motor with a large ceiling fan in place of a propeller. Four thick nylon cables attached the car to the baggoon.

When Astrid climbed in beside her mother, she discovered she had pedals. Everyone had pedals. They were like bicycle pedals except they were all joined together along a shaft. There were two more sets in the front, where her father was strapping himself in beside Dr Hu.

Lukas made Marie Curie jump over into the back. Then he pulled a small case marked 'Pre-flight

---

[15] I'm not sure about the ones on the other side – you'll have to ask the illustrator.

Safety Demonstration' from under the seat and walked round to the front of the car.

'Ladies and gentleman,' Dr Hu said, 'please give the cabin crew your full attention while he demonstrates the safety features of the baggoon.'

It was just like in an aeroplane. Lukas demonstrated how to fasten and unfasten their seat belts, how to make sure their seats were in the upright position, where the nearest exits were, and how to use their life jackets. (When he blew the little whistle for attracting attention in the ocean, Marie Curie became very excited and sprayed everyone with a fresh shower of drool.) He even pointed out the sick-bags.

'I hope we won't need those!' said Richard, joking.

'So do I,' said Dr Hu, not joking.

Finally, Lukas asked the passengers to switch off all their electrical equipment and mobile phones, and prepare for take-off.

'That was so embarrassing!' he whispered squeakily to Astrid as he climbed in beside her. His face was as pink as a rose.[16] 'When I grow up I definitely am *not* going to be a flight attendant.'

'I thought you were terr– [17]' Astrid began, but she was interrupted by the sudden roar of the outboard motor behind her.

'Sorry about the noise, ladies and gentlemen,' Dr Hu shouted. 'I'm afraid we have a bit of a

---

[16] I mean a *pink* rose this time – not a red one, a yellow one, a white one, or one of those orange-and-red stripey ones.
[17] Terrible? Terrifying? Pterodactyl? Your guess is as good as mine.

headwind today, so I have been forced to activate our auxiliary power system. Our estimated flight time is approximately 30 minutes. Please sit back and enjoy your flight.'

Then he pulled a lever on the dashboard and the Holden began to rattle and lurch and tremble.

'Wh-wh-what's g-g-going o-o-on?' gasped Astrid. 'I-i-is i-i-it a-a-an e-e-earthquake?'

'Th-th-that's ju-ju-just th-th-the fi-fi-fizzifier,' explained Lukas.

'Th-th-the fi-fi-fizzifier?'

'Th-th-that th-th-thing o-o-on th-th-the roo-roo-roof. I-i-it ma-ma-makes u-u-us fl-fl-fly.'

And they *were* flying! When Astrid looked out the window, she saw they were ten metres above the ground.

'La-la-ladies a-a-and ge-ge-gentlem-m-men,' bellowed Dr Hu. 'S-s-start pe-pe-pedalling.'

So much for sitting back and enjoying the flight, Astrid thought, putting her feet to the pedals.

10. Regnig

It was only five minutes as the crow flies from the railway station to the laboratory. But Dr Hu took them the long way. Well, the wind probably had something to do with it: it was blowing from the south-west and they were heading south-west. Figure it out.

Finally, after half an hour's frantic pedalling

by everyone except Marie Curie (there were no pedals in the back of the station wagon, just a pile of old roofing insulation to deaden the noise from the outboard motor[18]), Dr Hu turned off the fizzifier and brought the baggoon safely back to earth.

They landed in the railway car park.

'Ladies and gentlemen,' puffed their red-faced and badly shaken pilot. 'Thank you for flying Baggoon Airways. Your cabin crew and I hope you enjoyed your flight.'

'But we're right back where we started!' puffed Astrid's green-faced[19] and badly shaken mother.

Dr Hu nodded. 'I did warn you about the headwind.'

'So how do we get to your laboratory?' puffed Astrid's green-faced[20] and badly shaken father.

'I'm afraid we'll have to walk.'

Dr Hu tied a tow rope to the Holden's front bumper and the five of them dragged the baggoon back to the laboratory. It took half an hour. Three crows, who obviously had 25 minutes to spare, hitched a ride on the outboard motor.

'There are still some minor propulsion problems to work out,' Dr Hu admitted, as he hitched the Holden securely to a gum tree in front of the laboratory. 'But once they're sorted, the baggoon will be the most environmentally friendly means of transport since the invention of feet.'

'What about the gas, Doctor?' asked Jacqui.

'What gas, Doctor?'

---

[18] It didn't work.
[19] Those sick-bags *had* been useful, after all.
[20] See footnote 19.

'The gas in the baggoon.'

'It isn't gas,' he said. 'It's ginger beer.'

'Ginger beer!' Jacqui looked flummoxed.[21]

'Ginger beer!' Richard looked confounded, bewildered and disconcerted.

'Ginger beer!' Astrid looked thirsty. (Pedalling a baggoon for half an hour, then dragging it for *another* half an hour, is hot work.) 'Can we have some?'

'I'm afraid not,' Dr Hu said. 'This isn't normal ginger beer. Do you notice anything strange about the bubbles, Astrid?'

She squinted up at the huge, golden baggoon. 'They're going down, not up.'

He nodded. 'I was experimenting with different varieties of ginger plants, trying to find one that produced burpless ginger beer, when I accidentally stumbled across regnig.'

'What's regnig?'

'It's a very rare strain of ginger that works in reverse.'

'I get it,' said Astrid. 'Back-to-front ginger beer!'

'*Upside-down* ginger beer, actually,' Dr Hu said with a smile. 'The bubbles go down, the ginger beer goes up. It's the upside-down fizz that makes the baggoon fly.'

'Tell me, Doctor,' said Astrid's still-slightly-green-faced father, 'what was the point of all that shaking?'

The scientist pointed to the giant cocktail shaker on top of the Holden. 'After a while the

[21] **flummoxed** *adj*. confounded, bewildered, disconcerted.

ginger beer loses its fizz. I have to give it a bit of a shake to make it fizzy again.'

'Is it burpless?' asked Astrid.

'Well, ye-e-e-es,' Dr Hu said slowly.

Lukas leaned sideways. 'It makes you fart,' he whispered in Astrid's ear. Well, he meant to whisper, but his voice rasped (loudly) at exactly the wrong moment. The only thing the others heard was, 'FART.'

It nearly deafened Astrid.

Dr Hu quickly changed the subject. 'Would anyone like some morning tea?'

Unfortunately the subject didn't stay changed for long. Before anyone could answer, a raspy voice said (*very* loudly), 'FART!'

Everyone looked at Lukas, who turned as red as a rose.[22] 'It wasn't me!' he squeaked.

From right above Astrid's head, there came a squeaky echo. 'It wasn't me!'

Everyone looked up. On a branch of the gum tree sat a scruffy pink galah.

'Hullo,' Astrid said to it. 'You can talk!'

'Hullo,' said the galah, fluffing out its feathers and bobbing its head up and down. 'Hullo, hullo, hullo, hullo.'

'It must be someone's pet,' said Lukas. 'I wonder where it came from?'

'FART!' shouted the galah.

Dr Hu quickly changed the subject. 'Would anyone like some morning tea?

11. Domino effect

The Hus lived in a two-storey house right behind the laboratory. Mrs Hu had made date scones, but none of the visitors were hungry, for some reason.

'We'll just have a glass of water, thanks,' they said.

Dr Hu was spooning cream onto his third date scone. 'I was like that after my first baggoon flight,' he said, licking a blob of strawberry jam off his moustache. 'Couldn't keep anything down for 24 hours afterwards. Would anyone like some more cream?'

After morning tea, the scientist took his visitors across to his laboratory. Using a large whiteboard, he explained his theory.

First he drew the Earth, then he drew a thick orange circle around it.

'This is the ozone layer,' he said. 'It's a gas made from oxygen that provides a barrier between us and the harmful ultraviolet radiation from the sun.'

'Sort of like a natural sunscreen surrounding Earth,' Lukas squeaked.

'I *know* that,' Astrid whispered back. Did he think she was three years old?

'In the last half century,' Dr Hu was saying, 'man-made gases called CFCs and halons have been floating up into the atmosphere, causing a chemical reaction that attacks the ozone molecules, breaking them down and turning...'

Astrid yawned. It was like listening to her mother explain how she could fix things. 'Where do you go to school, Lukas?' she asked softly.

'Hakea Heights Secondary. I should be there now, but I had a bad asthma attack this morning. What about you?'

'Eucalyptus Hole.' She didn't say Eucalyptus Hole *Primary* School because she didn't want Lukas to know she was only in Grade 6. 'Mum and Dad said I didn't have to go today. This is more important.'

'If it's more important,' her father whispered, 'you should be listening.'

'I am listening,' Astrid said. To prove it, she asked Dr Hu a question. 'Where's the hole in the ozone layer?'

The scientist used one of the sleeves of his white laboratory coat to rub away a section of the orange circle right down at the bottom. 'Over Antarctica.'

'It's big!' Astrid gasped.

'Three times the size of Australia. And the problem isn't just confined to the South Pole,' Dr Hu said. 'The rest of the ozone layer is becoming progressively thinner.' Again using his sleeve, the scientist reduced the thickness of the entire orange circle. 'Since the 1960s, the risk of contracting skin cancer from the sun's rays has risen by more than 30 per cent.'

Astrid stared wide-eyed at the thin orange circle that represented the ozone layer. The problem was worse – and much, much bigger – than she had realised. It was *too* big.

Her father must have been thinking the same thing. 'Doctor, how can Astrid possibly make a difference?'

Dr Hu drew a tiny baggoon at the edge of the hole in the ozone layer. 'I plan to take her up there.'

'But the phenomenon is worldwide, Doctor. Even supposing that Astrid *can* fix the damaged ozone, you would have to fly her right around, and all over, the globe. It would take years and years!'

'Not if my theory is correct,' said Dr Hu. 'You see, Mr and Dr Spark, I believe that your daughter might be able to start a domino effect. All she has to do is use the magnetic ability of her fingers to *begin* the repair process,' – with a fresh orange marker, he made a small scribble at the edge of the ozone hole – 'and that will set in motion a chemical reaction that will spread right around the world.' *Scribble, scribble, scribble.* Starting at the South Pole, a thick orange band representing the repaired ozone layer soon surrounded the planet.

'QED[23],' said Dr Hu, smiling and spreading his arms wide (one of his sleeves was bright orange). 'Everyone lives happily ever after!'

12. Unhappily ever after

'It'll never work,' squeaked Lukas.

They all looked at him.

'It's really cold in the upper atmosphere,' he rasped, his words whistling through his crooked teeth. 'You and Astrid will freeze.'

'I'll devise a heating system,' said his father, and wrote, *'Heating system,'* on the whiteboard.

---

[23] What scientists (and maths teachers) say when they're showing off.

'The ginger beer will freeze.'

Dr Hu wrote, '*Heating system x 2*.'

'You'll need to pressurise the cabin.'

Dr Hu wrote, '*Pressurise cabin*.'

'There's a lot of rust in the station wagon, Dad. It probably won't take the pressure.'

Dr Hu sighed. 'You're right, Lukas. I'll have to buy a stronger car.' He wrote, '*Volvo?*'

'And you'll need a bigger baggoon,' squeaked Lukas. 'A Volvo with all that equipment in it would be lots heavier than our old station wagon.'

'*Bigger baggoon*,' wrote his father.

'With lots more ginger beer.'

Dr Hu added '*More ginger beer*' to the list. He turned around. 'Is there anything else, Lukas?'

'I don't think so.'

'Well, thank heavens for that!' Dr Hu drew a line beneath the list.

'It still won't work,' rasped Lukas.

His father closed his eyes. 'Why not, Lukas?'

'Think about it, Dad. If you can't even fly from the railway station to here, how do you expect to get all the way to the South Pole?'

'I don't need to go to the South Pole. The hole opens and closes depending on the time of year. When it's at its largest, it reaches halfway to Australia.'

'That's still a long way,' Lukas squeaked.

Dr Hu used his orange sleeve to rub out the line on the whiteboard, then he added '*New propulsion system*' to the list.

'A new propulsion system would probably be heavier than the one on the Holden,' rasped Lukas.

'*MORE ginger beer*,' wrote his father.

'How high is the ozone layer, Dad?'

'It starts at about 19,000 metres.'

'Can a baggoon fly that high?'

Dr Hu ran his fingers through his hair. He looked much older than he had two minutes ago. 'I must confess,' he admitted in a low, dispirited voice, 'that I'm not really sure.'

Astrid glared at Lukas. She decided she didn't like him very much any more. 'Of course it'll go high enough,' she said.

'How do you know?' Lukas rasped.

'Girl's intuition.'

'I'm afraid girl's intuition isn't enough, Astrid,' said Dr Hu. He glanced round at the whiteboard and sighed. 'Lukas is right. It looks as though I still have quite a bit of work ahead of me.'

13. Not the Voovl!

'You know, Doctor,' Jacqui said as they all walked outside, '*we've* got an old Volvo. You can have that, if you like.'

'Why, that's very kind of you, Doctor.'

Astrid turned to her mother. 'You don't mean the Voovl[24]!'

'Voovl?' Dr Hu sounded puzzled.

---

[24] **Voovl** *n*. How a three-year-old Astrid spells Volvo. (For more about the Voovl, see *Echidna Mania*, available at a bookshop near you.)

'It's a long story,' said Jacqui.[25]

'But Mum,' Astrid said, 'you *can't* give away the Voovl!'

'It's for a good cause.'

'I know that. But the Voovl's part of the family!'

'We don't need two cars,' said Jacqui. 'The Voovl hardly ever gets used.'

'Felix uses it.'

'Felix is hardly ever home, darling.'

Astrid cringed. She hated being called darling in front of other people – especially boys. 'He's coming back next month.'

'Only for a week. Then he's off on his European tour.'

'Look, if there's any problem...,' Dr Hu began. And stopped – stopped talking *and* stopped walking. His face turned suddenly pale.

'Where's the baggoon?'

It was gone. In the tree where it had been tethered sat a scruffy pink galah with a short length of chewed rope dangling from its beak.

'Hullo,' it said sweetly.
'Like some morning tea?
Like some morning tea?'

Dr Hu shook his fist at it.
'What have you done, you pesky bird?'

'It wasn't me. It wasn't me. It wasn't me.'

'Look!' Lukas cried.

The galah dropped the rope and bobbed its head

    26,471 words long, to be exact.

up and down. 'Look!' it screeched. 'Look! Look! Look! Look!'

Everyone ignored the galah as best they could and looked up to where Lukas was pointing. High overhead, a tiny baggoon-and-car-shaped speck floated up towards the ozone layer.

Dr Hu let out a big sigh. 'Well, I'm very sorry, Dr Spark, Mr Spark, Astrid – but it looks as though you might have to walk back to the railway station.'

'That's okay,' Astrid said, trying not to look too relieved. 'At least we won't have to pull a baggoon this time.'

14. The next baggoon

When they arrived home that evening there was a message from Kia-Jane asking Astrid to phone her.

'How's your boyfriend?' was the first thing she said.

'He is *not* my boyfriend!' Astrid retorted. Luckily Kia-Jane wasn't there to see her face turn as pink as a rose.[26] 'How was school?'

'Same as always,' said Kia-Jane. 'I want to know about *your* day, Super Glue. What happened? Did you fix the ozone layer? Can we throw away our hats and sunscreen forever? Are they going to make you a Knight of the Empire, award you the Nobel Prize, put your face on a postage stamp? Do I have to curtsey to you from now on?'

'Yes,' Astrid said, 'you have to curtsey. But "no" to all the other questions.'

She told Kia-Jane everything that had happened. (Well, nearly everything – she left out the bit where Lukas gave her something just before they said goodbye.[27]) Then she mentioned that she and her mother were driving the Voovl up to Hakea Heights on the weekend.

'Can I come?' asked Kia-Jane.

'I guess so. If it's okay with your mum and dad. You'll need money for the train fare back.'

'Huh? Are you and your mum staying there?'

'No, the Voovl is,' Astrid said. 'We're donating it. It's going to become part of the next baggoon.'

Kia-Jane laughed. 'I wonder where the old one ended up?'

15. Off the planet

Six hundred kilometres overhead, a cosmonaut[28] and an astronaut[29] were involved in a joint Russian-American experiment to see whether men could live for a year up in space. Only three days after their arrival at the International Space Station, they observed something very strange through one of the portholes. The cosmonaut went out to investigate. When he returned, the astronaut helped him remove his bulky helmet.

'Well, Major Vladimir, what did you discover?'

---

[27] I left that bit out, too.

[28] **cosmonaut** n. a Russian astronaut.

[29] **astronaut** n. an American cosmonaut.

'It is a balloon, Colonel Randy,' said the cosmonaut.

'No way, Vladdy-baby!' The American punched his Russian colleague playfully on the arm. 'You're kidding me, right?'

'These American jokes I am not understanding,' Major Vladimir said, frowning and rubbing his arm. 'It is a balloon for sure, Baby Randy, one hundred per cent.'

'But . . . but . . .' Colonel Randy stammered, 'it's physically impossible for a balloon to make it this far from Earth.'

'Okay, but a balloon most definitely it is,' said Major Vladimir. 'And to this balloon is connected a most strange thing. Look, Colonel Randy – I have some photographs snipped.'

Colonel Randy peered at the tiny screen on the back of Major Vladimir's digital camera, and his eyes grew very large. 'Vladimir, that's a *station wagon*!'

'For sure, it is family car, yes?'

The American nodded. 'Was there anybody . . . aboard?'

'One hundred per cent,' said Major Vladimir. He couldn't stop himself from grinning. 'But for sure you are thinking this is Russian joke. So I have for you, Colonel Randy, something to show.'

With that, the cosmonaut space-walked over to the airlock and pulled the door wide open. Moments later, Colonel Randy was knocked floating by a huge brown-and-white Saint Bernard.

16. On the planet

'I don't know *where* she is,' rasped Lukas, standing at the door holding a large, nearly overflowing bowl of dog food. 'It's like she's disappeared completely off the face the Earth.'

17. The chapter before the next one

Even though she wasn't *supposed* to charge people for fixing things, at school Astrid sometimes accepted 'donations' in exchange for her services.

Her rates were very reasonable: two dollars for bends, dents, cracks, and for things that had snapped cleanly in two; five dollars if there were three or more pieces, for all glassware and most electrical items; ten dollars for computers, pushbikes, mobile phones and for just about anything that had been accidentally put through the wash, dropped from a tall building, or run over by a steamroller.

Astrid didn't really *like* accepting money, but Kia-Jane (who acted as her manager and kept 50 per cent) said it was a human relations issue: if Astrid *didn't* charge for fixing things, she would be teaching the other children, particularly those in the lower grades, to exploit her. And that, said Kia-Jane, would be setting a bad example.

But Astrid had never been offered money by a teacher. Until the chapter after the next one.

18. One hat, two hats, red hat, blue hat...

Ms Chapeau, Astrid's art teacher, was known as the Mad Hatter (behind her back[30]) because she always wore hats. Even on cloudy days. Even on windy days. Even inside. She had millions of them.

There were big hats, small hats,
low hats, tall hats,
mop hats, top hats,
cop hats and bebop hats;
There were shiny hats, spiny hats,
huge hats, tiny hats,
lacy hats, racy hats,
spacey hats
and Dick Tracy hats;
There were hard hats, soft hats,
guard hats, doffed hats,
tight hats, loose hats,
and zany Dr Seuss hats;
There were hats with strings,
hats with wings,
hats with feathers,
and hats for all weathers;
There were hats with flowers,
hats with towers (of things on top of them),
and hats you could look at
for hours and hours;
There were hats of fake fur,
hats of fake snakeskin,

---

[30] Or whispered, really quietly, down the back of the classroom.

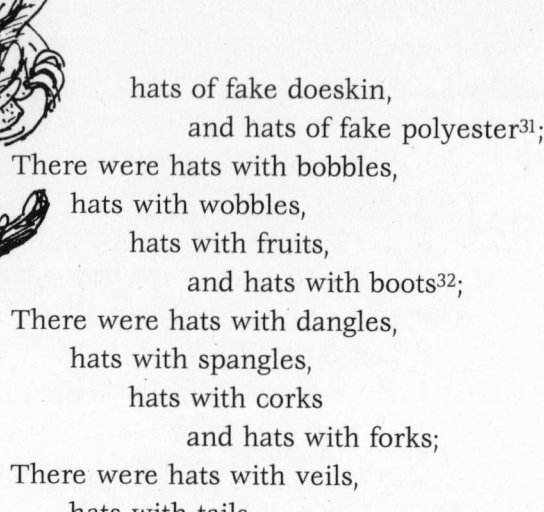

hats of fake doeskin,
and hats of fake polyester[31];
There were hats with bobbles,
hats with wobbles,
hats with fruits,
and hats with boots[32];
There were hats with dangles,
hats with spangles,
hats with corks
and hats with forks;
There were hats with veils,
hats with tails,
elastic hats
and fantastic hats;

And then there were lots of other hats
that *didn't* rhyme: boaters, beanies, berets,
balaclavas, cloches, fezzes, fedoras, pith
helmets, tam-o'-shanters, turbans, topees,
toques, trilbies, baseball hats, cowgirl hats,
nurses' hats, pork-pie hats, race-day hats,
thinking hats, Mad Hatter hats, sun hats,
rain hats, cloudy-day hats, witches' hats,
paper hats, tin hats, gauze hats, straw hats
and still more hats.

[31] Actually, they might have been real polyester.
[32] Well, they *matched* her boots.

And every hat,
      without exception,
           was worn just once;
                Ohhhhh, what a collection!
In short, Ms Chapeau wore a different hat to school every day.[33]

19. Split ends

The day after Astrid's first trip to Hakea Heights, the Mad Hatter approached her in the schoolyard. The art teacher was wearing a Mexican sombrero that cast a huge shadow, so when Ms Chapeau came up behind her, Astrid thought the baggoon had been found and was paying her school a surprise visit. She cringed, expecting a rain of dog drool to come slopping down on her, and perhaps to hear Lukas's squeaky-raspy voice, but instead she heard the Mad Hatter say, very sternly, 'Astrid Spark, would you come with me, please.'

Astrid nervously followed the Mad Hatter across the yard to the art room, wondering all the way what she had done. Was it the hat (a very large Mexican sombrero) she had drawn on her painting of the Mona Lisa that morning? But people were always drawing hats, or sculpting hats, or lino-cutting hats, or weaving hats, or making clay-model hats in art, and nobody had ever got into trouble over it before.

When they reached the art room the Mad

[33] I know what you're thinking – I could have saved time (and a couple of pages) and said that at the beginning of the chapter, but then you might never have found out what a talented poet I am.

Hatter closed and locked the door behind them. 'Astrid,' she said, her voice lowered to a whisper, 'I need your help.'

Astrid breathed a sigh of relief. 'What is it, Ms Chapeau?'

The Mad Hatter glanced furtively around the room. Then she pulled something from her pocket and stuffed it into Astrid's hand.

It was a fifty-dollar note!

'What's this for, Ms Chapeau?'

'Sssssssh! Not so loud!' hissed the Mad Hatter. She darted over to the window and lowered the blinds. 'I want you to fix something for me.'

'Okay,' Astrid said. 'But I'm not really supposed to accept money.'

'It can be our secret.'

Astrid pocketed the money guiltily. Fifty dollars was way too much! 'What do you want me to fix?'

The Mad Hatter rattled the door to make sure it was properly locked. Then she slowly turned around and, taking a deep breath, she removed her hat.

SPROINGGGG!

Astrid couldn't help herself – she let out a gasp.

'Terrible, isn't it?' Ms Chapeau said sadly. 'Now you know why I always wear hats.'

Her head was surrounded by what looked like a huge cloud of golden fairy floss. It was a metre across and went up nearly to the ceiling.

'Is that your . . . *hair*?' Astrid asked.

Ms Chapeau nodded her huge woolly head.

'I had an accident several years ago – a bad electric shock – and it split every one of my hairs into ten!'

It was the worst case of split ends Astrid had ever seen. 'Have you tried conditioner, Ms Chapeau?'

'I've tried *everything*! I even tried shaving it all off. But it always grows back like this,' Ms Chapeau said. 'Please, Astrid Spark, please fix my split ends!'

Astrid felt sorry for her. But there was nothing she could do. 'I'm not allowed to fix people.'

'What do you mean, *not allowed*?'

'It's a rule,' Astrid explained. 'I tried fixing someone once and it was a disaster.[34] Since then Mum and Dad say I'm only allowed to fix *things*, never people or animals.'

'I won't tell your parents,' said the art teacher.

'But something could go wrong, Ms Chapeau. Fixology isn't something you can control. I put my fingers on something and think fixing thoughts, and the molecules rearrange or join or whatever. But sometimes they don't rearrange or join in the right way. I might make you *worse*!'

Ms Chapeau pointed up at her fairy-floss hair. 'What could be worse than this?'

Astrid could think of one thing.[35] 'All right,' she said finally. 'But if something goes wrong, will you promise not to be cross with me?'

'I promise,' said Ms Chapeau.

---

34 For more about this, see 'Chapter 76: Mrs Hudson's Bottom' in *Echidna Mania*, available at a bookshop near you.

35 See footnote 34.

Astrid asked her to sit in a chair. 'Your hair really is amazing,' she said, touching it hesitantly with the tips of her fixologist's fingers.

'It used to be beautiful,' Ms Chapeau said wistfully, a dreamy look crossing her face. She leaned back and closed her eyes. 'Before my accident, I was on shampoo ads on TV. Wherever I went, people would comment on how lovely my hair was. Now I'm embarrassed to be seen without a hat.'

For nearly five minutes there was complete silence in the art room as Astrid combed her fingers through Ms Chapeau's hair and thought fixing thoughts. Finally she stepped back and said, 'All done!'

The former Mad Hatter opened her eyes. With trembling hands she reached up and felt her long, sleek tresses of healthy, lustrous, gorgeous, to-die-for, 100-per-cent-split-ends-free hair.

'Astrid, thank you, thank you!' she sobbed, hugging her. As she was being hugged, Astrid slipped the fifty dollars back into Ms Chapeau's pocket. 'Now I won't have to wear hats ever again!' the teacher said.

'But Ms Chapeau,' Astrid told her, very sternly, 'you might get skin cancer!'

20. Gained a galah

Astrid, her mother and Kia-Jane were having lunch at the Hus' house. They had just driven down from Eucalyptus Hole to deliver the Voovl.

'Marie Curie isn't the kind of dog that would run away,' Lukas said in his squeaky, raspy voice.

Astrid stared at Lukas's teeth as he talked. They were so very crooked. After her success with Ms Chapeau's hair, she wondered if...?

Then she remembered that she didn't like Lukas very much. And, anyway, her mother was there, and so were both Lukas's parents and his big sister, Brittany. And so was Kia-Jane.

'Someone might have dog-napped her,' Kia-Jane said.

Mrs Hu set her knife and fork down. 'Why would anyone *dog*-nap Marie Curie?'

'For ransom. After all, she is quite famous.'

'Since when was Marie Curie famous?' asked Brittany.

'Since she won the Nobel Prize,' said Kia-Jane.

Dr Hu looked at her seriously. 'We haven't received a ransom note.'

'Maybe the dog-nappers can't write.'

Now *everyone* looked at Kia-Jane.

'Well,' she said, 'there are lots of people who can't read and write. Maybe they dog-napped Marie Curie so they could get the money to do a TAFE course and *learn* to write ransom notes!'

'Are there courses that teach that?' asked Lukas.

'No, dummy,' his big sister said. 'She's only joking.'

Lukas turned pink as a rose[36] and Astrid (despite not liking him very much) couldn't help feeling just a tiny bit sorry for him.

[36] See footnote 26.

'I think *I* know what happened to Marie Curie,' she said. 'Did anyone remember to take her out of the Holden last Sunday?'

'Oops!' squawked Lukas, going pinker still.

'Oops!' squawked the galah, perfectly camouflaged in the rose bush[37] outside the kitchen window.

'Look on the bright side,' Kia-Jane said cheerfully. 'You've lost your dog, but you've gained a galah.'

Strange, but that didn't seem to cheer anyone up.

EXCEPT ME.

21. Lost

LOST
120 kg Saint Bernard dog.
Good with children.
Last seen 2,000 metres above
Hakea Heights, heading east.
Reward offered.

---

[37] It had pink roses – not red ones, yellow ones, white ones, or those orange-and-red stripey ones.

22. Found

How good is your memory?

Cast your mind back to Chapter 5. When they met for the first time, did you notice that Dr Hu said he was an admirer of Astrid's mother's work? Perhaps you wondered about that.

The reason he knew about her work was quite simple. Dr Jacqui Spark was famous. Several years earlier (when Astrid was three), her mother discovered aliens. Actually, it was a man called William Richardson who discovered them, but it was Astrid's mother who worked out what they were. Jacqui was an astrophysicist and aliens were her specialty. She knew more about aliens than anyone *except* aliens. But that's another story.[38] There aren't any aliens in this one. Only an astronaut, a cosmonaut, and an astrodog. There's also an astrophysicist, of course, because that was still Jacqui's job.

She worked in an observatory at the top of Mount Stringybark, 50 kilometres from where the Sparks lived. Two or three times a week she would drive up there and spend the whole night looking up into the sky through giant telescopes. Sometimes, on weekends or in the holidays, Astrid was allowed to go with her. Astrid quite enjoyed looking at the stars, and there was a bed in the little staffroom where she could sleep when she grew tired. There was a couch there as well – that's where Kia-Jane slept when she was allowed to come.

---

[38] It's called *Echidna Mania* (and you already know where to find it).

Both girls were there the following weekend. But they weren't in bed.[39] They were taking turns using one of the giant telescopes. Kia-Jane was sitting in the observer's chair and Astrid was operating the controls that moved the telescope from side to side.

'A little bit to the left,' Kia-Jane was saying. 'Bit more ... bit more ... bit more ... Stop!'

Astrid yawned. It was nearly midnight. 'C'mon, Kia-Jane, you've had long enough. Give me a go.'

'Wait a sec.' Kia-Jane's eye was jammed up against the viewing lens. 'I can see something.'

'Of course you can see something,' Astrid said. 'There's a whole universe out there.'

'But this looks like a window.'

'A *window*?'

'Well, it's more like a porthole, actually. With a bit of paper taped to the inside of the glass. There's writing on it.' Kia-Jane adjusted the magnification knob. 'But I can't quite make it out ...'

'Give me a look,' Astrid said.

Kia-Jane moved aside and Astrid climbed into the observer's chair. 'Wow!' she breathed.

It seemed to be a message of some kind.

НАЙДЕНА
Одна очень большая собака.
Хорошо относится к космонавтам.
Обращайтесь за справками внутри.

[39] Or on couch.

'It must be an alien language,' said Astrid.

'*Alien!*' Jacqui was right across the other side of the observatory, but she had those radar ears.

'Let me see,' she cried, breaking the world speed record for crossing observatories.[40]

Astrid and Kia-Jane stood by excitedly while Jacqui peered through the telescope.

'Well?' Astrid couldn't bear the suspense any longer. 'Is it a message from aliens, Mum?'

'No,' said Jacqui, increasing the magnification. 'I think it's Russian. Get me a pen and paper, please.'

Jacqui copied the message down. Then she hurried across to the fax machine and dialled the number of a Russian astrophysicist she knew.

Twenty minutes later, a translation came spitting out of the printer: *Found. One very large dog. Good with cosmonauts. Apply within.*

'What does it mean?' asked Astrid.

'It means,' Jacqui said slowly, 'that Dr Hu's ginger beer baggoons are certainly capable of flying as high as the ozone layer.'

23. Playing fetch

'Dog food?' said the radio operator at Mission Control. 'Did I hear you correctly, Colonel Randy?'

'Affirmative,' said Colonel Randy. 'We need tons of the stuff. And flea powder,' he added, reaching inside his spacesuit to scratch an itch. 'Please send them on the very next supply ship.'

---

[40] Set way back in 1908 by the fleet of foot, though clumsy, English astronomer, Tripson C. Stars.

Across the other side of the space station, Major
Vladimir and the astrodog were playing fetch with a
badly chewed, drool-covered piece of footwear.

'I also need a new pair of slippers,' Colonel
Randy added.

24. Lost dog/found dog

Next morning Astrid phoned Lukas, who told his
father, who phoned Mission Control, who patched
the call through to the International Space Station.

Major Vladimir: 'Who is calling, please?'

Dr Hu: 'Dr Hu.'

Major Vladimir: 'You are *real*?'

Dr Hu (after a short pause): 'Well, I *think* I'm
real.'

Major Vladimir: 'I thought you were just the
character on the TV.'

Dr Hu: 'I'm not the TV Dr Who, I'm the book
Dr Hu.'

Major Vladimir: 'How can I help you, Mr Book
Dr Hu?'

Mr Book Dr Hu: 'It's about the lost dog.'

Major Vladimir: 'What lost dog?'

Dr Hu: 'I understood you found a dog.'

Major Vladimir: 'We have found a dog, most definitely.'

Dr Hu: 'Well, that's the one I'm calling about.'

Major Vladimir: 'I am being most confused. You said *lost* dog, not found dog.'

Dr Hu (after another short pause): 'Sorry. I meant the found dog. I believe it belongs to my son. She's been a family pet for nearly ten years.'

Major Vladimir: 'Your son he is coming to collect his found dog?'

Dr Hu: 'Well, that could be difficult. You see, we live in Australia and we don't have access to any spacecraft at the moment. We were wondering if you could look after her for us until we find a way to bring her back.'

Major Vladimir: 'For sure I am looking after her. She is very excellent dog. When I am returning to Earth next year I am making sure your son gets back his found dog.'

25. 423,156 green bottles

It took Dr Hu six months to build the bagggoon.

'That's bagggoon with three Gs,' he said, in case someone was writing a book about it.[41] The third G was for extra lift.

'Brewing all that ginger beer was the most time-consuming part,' he explained. 'Have you any idea how many bottles it takes to fill a bagggoon that size?'

Astrid, her parents and Kia-Jane craned their necks. The bagggoon was three times the size of the baggoon. It towered over Dr Hu's laboratory, filling half the sky (the other half was filled with dirty brown smog from the city).

'One,' said Kia-Jane.

Everyone looked at her.

'Well, you could use the same bottle over and over.'

'Ha ha!' squawked Lukas. (Or it might have been the galah. Their voices were very similar.)

'Ha ha!' squawked the galah. (Or it might have been Lukas. Their voices were very similar.)

Meanwhile, Jacqui's forehead was creased in concentration. She was working it out.

'423,156 bottles,' she said at last.

Dr Hu smirked. 'You have underestimated by some 1,844 bottles, Dr Spark.'

'Did you lose any ginger beer through popped corks, Dr Hu?' asked Jacqui.

'Well, yes, as a matter of fact I did. And quite a few bottles simply flew away.'

It was Jacqui's turn to smirk. 'I think you will find that accounts for the disparity.'

'Go, Dr Spark!' Kia-Jane whispered.

Astrid was still admiring the bagggoon. 'Is it ready to go, Dr Hu?'

'Very nearly,' he said. 'I want to take it for a test flight first.'

'A test flight?' said Richard, who had missed an important lawyers' meeting that morning because of Dr Hu's phone call. 'Why did you ask us to come all the way down here today, Doctor, if you're only making a test flight?'

'Because it's a dress rehearsal for the real thing,' said Dr Hu, who had missed an important scientists' meeting to test the bagggoon, 'so I need Astrid to accompany me.'

'How long will the test flight take, Doctor?' asked Jacqui, who had an important astrophysicists' meeting at four o'clock that afternoon.

'Ten or twelve hours,' Dr Hu said. He glanced at his watch. 'I'm afraid it's too late to go up today. Never mind, we can try again tomorrow.'

'Tomorrow?' Richard wailed. 'I can't miss two days' work!'

'Neither can I,' said Jacqui.

'Can I come down by myself then?' asked Astrid. It was the school holidays and *she* wasn't missing any important meetings.

'Well . . .' Her parents looked at each other.

'I can catch the train by myself.'

'Well . . .' said her father.

'I'll be thirteen next birthday.'

'Well . . .' said her mother.

'I'll come along and keep her company,' Kia-Jane volunteered.

'Well . . .' said the galah.

'I've got it!' squeaked Lukas. 'Astrid, why don't you and Kia-Jane stay at our place tonight?'

26. Not even a scar

Brittany Hu was in her last year of high school. She was supposed to be studying for exams. Astrid, Kia-Jane and Lukas could hear her in her bedroom playing CDs while they did the dinner dishes that night.

'Is your brother really in a band, Astrid?' Lukas rasped.

'He's the drummer with Echidna.'

'They're wicked! I wish I could meet him.'

'He's overseas at the moment,' Astrid said. 'But I'll invite you down next time he's home.'

'That'd be really cool, Astrid.'

Kia-Jane began humming a popular love song, until Astrid elbowed her in the ribs.

'Lukas,' Kia-Jane asked, 'do you have a girlfriend?'

Lukas went pink as a rose[42] (or a galah), took a couple of big, gasping breaths and said, 'Uh-oh!'

Then he doubled over in a coughing fit.

'Lukas, are you okay?' Astrid asked.

He shook his head. 'As . . . thma!' he gasped, between coughs. Dropping his tea towel, he fumbled in his pockets, found a ventolin puffer and squirted it into his mouth. *Huff! Huff! Huff!* he breathed noisily. 'That's . . . better.'

42 See footnote 36.

His breathing was better, but not his foot. All three of them noticed it at the same time. They saw the blood first, then the steak-knife – well, the *handle* of the steak-knife. The knife must have fallen out of the tea towel when Lukas dropped it. And buried itself, point-first, into his foot.

'Oh maaaan!' Lukas groaned, when he saw what had happened. He sank to the floor, his face suddenly as white as a sheet.[43]

Astrid felt sick. Bending down beside Lukas, clenching her teeth, she yanked the knife out of his foot. Then, thinking fixing thoughts without really realising it, she brushed the blood away from the wound. And brushed the wound away, too.

Lukas was breathing deeply, looking at his foot, his eyes wide, not in shock this time but in amazement. There wasn't even a scar.

Kia-Jane was first to recover. 'That'll be twenty dollars, Luko. We accept cash, IOUs and all major credit cards.'

'Huh?' Lukas rasped weakly.

'Super Glue's fee. And twenty dollars is a real bargain, believe me. A doctor would charge twice that, *and* there'd be stitches.'

Astrid helped Lukas to his feet. 'Ignore her.'

'Ignore your manager?' Kia-Jane tried to sound offended. 'Astrid, you have absolutely no idea how to run a business!'

---

[43] A *white* sheet – not a coloured one, or one with pretty patterns on it.

'*Mind* your own business,' Astrid told her. She bent down and picked up the steak-knife. 'I probably should wash this again.'

27. Excellence rating

'On an excellence rating,' Kia-Jane said, 'I'd put that up alongside the Mad Hatter's split ends.'

She and Astrid were lying awake in the Hus' spare bedroom late that night.

'It *was* pretty good, wasn't it?' said Astrid, holding her hands up so she could see her ten amazing fingers silhouetted against the stars outside the window. 'I wonder if I'll be able to fix the ozone layer.'

'Super Glue,' Kia-Jane said seriously, 'I reckon your fingers could fix anything.'

Astrid hoped she was right.

28. U-u-up u-u-up and a-a-away

The Voovl was almost unrecognisable. There were hair-dryers all over the car – hundreds of them! – all facing rearwards and all attached to special brackets that swivelled when you moved a joystick that had replaced the steering wheel. The hair-dryers worked like little jet engines to propel the car. (The Voovl's wheels had been removed and replaced with particularly powerful hair-dryers.) And the heat from the hair-dryers would rise up and prevent the ginger beer in the bagggoon from freezing. There were hair-dryers inside the Voovl, too – they worked as heaters to warm the car's interior. All the hair-dryers were powered by large solar-panels sticking out on each side of the car like square silver wings.

On the Voovl's roof was a brand new fizzifier – *twice* as big as the last one. (Just one look at it was enough to make Astrid's stomach feel queasy.) There was also a weird-looking periscope with a camcorder on the end.

Inside, the Voovl had been completely transformed. The back seats had been removed and replaced with gas cylinders, tanks, pumps, hair-dryers, compressors and a tangled spaghetti of hoses, cables, wires and pipes.

The front seats were surrounded by instruments, taps, levers, TV monitors and lots more hoses, cables, wires and pipes. But no pedals, Astrid was pleased to see. She buckled herself in.

'Good heavens!' Dr Hu muttered in the driver's seat.

The galah was sitting on one of the windscreen wipers.

'Clear off, you stupid bird!' Astrid cried.

'It can't hear you,' said Dr Hu. He switched on a microphone. 'Lukas, would you remove the bird from the wipers, please.'

There was a flurry of pink-and-grey feathers, then Lukas grinned through the windscreen. He gave them a thumbs-up.

'Are you ready for lift-off, Dad?'

'Roger that, Lukas. Would all personnel please clear the launch site.'

Lukas walked back towards Kia-Jane and his mother, who were both holding ropes, and then Dr Hu pushed a button. 'Engines on.'

There was a buzzing noise and a gentle vibration as 408 hair-dryers hummed into action.

Suddenly Brittany appeared outside Dr Hu's window. She had a towel wrapped around her head. 'Dad, have you seen my hair-dryer?'

Her father looked guilty. 'Um. Could you walk round behind the car and hold the rope, darling?' he asked. 'I'm sure your hair will be dry in no time.'

Dr Hu fiddled with a few more instruments, then he pulled a big lever.

'Activating the fizzifier,' he announced.

Uh-oh! thought Astrid.

There was a sloshing, swooshing noise from directly overhead and the Voovl began to lurch and bump and vibrate. Astrid had to grip the edges of her seat.

'Th-th-this i-i-is th-th-the bi-bi-bit I-I-I ha-ha-hate!' she grimaced.

'W-w-we wo-wo-won't nee-nee-need i-i-it fo-fo-for lo-lo-long,' said Dr Hu. 'Ju-ju-just t-t-to ge-ge-get u-u-us st-st-started.'

La-la-later, wh-wh-when th-th-the fi-fi-fizzifier wa-wa-was fi-fi-finally tur-tur-turned o-o-off, and they could talk properly again, Dr Hu explained that because the ginger beer in the bagggoon was brand new, it was still really fizzy and didn't need much shaking.

'It's only when it starts to go flat, or when we have extra passengers, that we need the fizzifier going all the time,' the scientist said, as the bagggoon soared up into the wide brown sky.

29. Pass

The higher they went, the colder it became, even though the day was sunny and cloudless.

At 4,000 metres, Dr Hu turned on the hair-dryers *inside* the Voovl. It reminded Astrid of something that had been puzzling her since Chapter 22. 'Dr Hu, how did Marie Curie stay warm?'

The scientist took 500 metres to ponder Astrid's question. Finally, at 4,500 metres, he said, 'There was a big pile of roofing insulation in the back of the Holden. She must have burrowed right into it.'

At 7,000 metres, Dr Hu turned on the auxiliary oxygen.

At 7,101 metres, Astrid asked, 'How did she breathe?'

At 7,146 metres, Dr Hu said, 'Lukas suffers from asthma. I had installed a small oxygen cylinder in the Holden in case we went too high and he found breathing difficult. My guess is the valve worked its way open, or Marie Curie somehow managed to open it herself.'

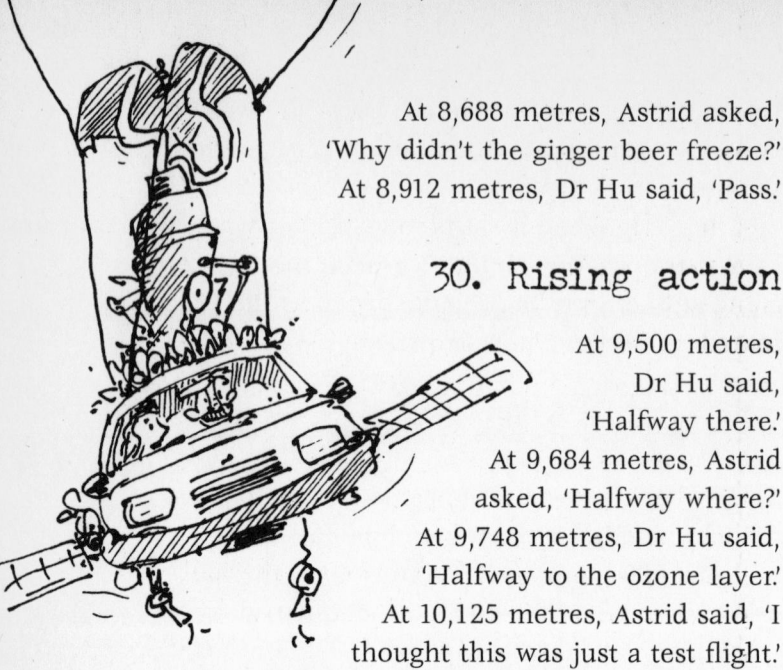

At 8,688 metres, Astrid asked,
'Why didn't the ginger beer freeze?'
At 8,912 metres, Dr Hu said, 'Pass.'

30. Rising action

At 9,500 metres,
Dr Hu said,
'Halfway there.'
At 9,684 metres, Astrid
asked, 'Halfway where?'
At 9,748 metres, Dr Hu said,
'Halfway to the ozone layer.'
At 10,125 metres, Astrid said, 'I
thought this was just a test flight.'
At 10,162 metres, Dr Hu said, 'It is.'

At 10,166 metres, Astrid said, 'We're still going up.'

At 10,173 metres, Dr Hu said, 'We won't go much higher than this.'

At 12,555 metres, Astrid said, 'I thought you said . . .'

At 12,555 metres, Dr Hu interrupted her. 'Take a look at this.'

31. Who knows?

For the whole of the last chapter, Dr Hu had been peering intently through the periscope, which poked down through the roof between the two seats. Now he let Astrid take a look.

She could see half of the bagggoon towering above them, and beyond that a big semicircle of sky. But everything looked weird.

'Why is the sky orange?' Astrid asked.

'That's the ozone layer,' Dr Hu said. 'Normally you wouldn't be able to see it, but that isn't a normal periscope – it's an ozonescope. I invented it myself. What you're looking at is the ozone layer. Rotate the scope to the left.'

Astrid moved the ozonescope around until the orange changed colour.

'It's gone blue,' she said.

'That's where the ozone stops and the hole starts,' said Dr Hu.

'Is that where we're going?'

'Not today,' Dr Hu said. 'It's much too far to the south of us. I'm hoping for a change of wind direction in a day or so.'

He turned a big brass tap on the dashboard and a loud hissing noise came from outside. Still gazing through the ozonescope, Astrid saw a stream of liquid come spilling out of a pipe on the side of the fizzifier. She began to panic.

'Doctor, we're losing ginger beer!'

'It's okay,' he said. 'I'm taking us back to earth.'

'But what about the ginger beer? We won't be able to fly without it!'

Dr Hu checked the altimeter, then adjusted the tap. 'Don't worry, I'm only releasing a small amount – just enough to begin our descent.'

Astrid watched the escaping ginger beer as it poured out of the pipe, splashing up over the sides of the bagggoon and spraying off into the orange sky above them.

'Where will it go?'

Dr Hu shrugged. 'Who knows?'

32. Major Vladimir knows

The cosmonaut came struggling back through the airlock. He was greeted by the astrodog, which knocked him helmet-over-boots and began enthusiastically licking him all over. The astronaut hauled the huge dog off his helpless colleague, then helped Major Vladimir remove his bulky helmet.

'You ought to teach your dog better manners, Vladimir,' laughed Colonel Randy. 'She's covered you in dog drool.'

'The dog has not been making this waters,' Major Vladimir said. 'It is raindrips.'

Colonel Randy laughed all the more. 'Vladdy-baby, you crack me up! You and your Russian humour! Ha ha ha ha!'

Major Vladimir still wasn't laughing. 'For sure, I am not joking, Baby Randy. It is raindrips, one hundred per cent.'

'Rain in space! Ha ha ha ha!' The astronaut laughed himself up to the ceiling. 'Rain in space! Vladdy-baby, you'll be the death of me.'

The Russian looked shocked. 'Baby Randy,

you are my comrade and friend. Never will I cause
for you to be dying.'

Colonel Randy couldn't speak. He laughed and
laughed. Finally Major Vladimir grabbed the
American's spacesuit and towed him over to a
porthole.

'For yourself, have a look, Colonel Randy. See,
it is outside making raindrips.'

The astronaut blinked the tears from his eyes
and looked out through the porthole. He blinked
again, and his mouth slowly dropped open. 'Well,
glory be! It really *is* raining!'

Major Vladimir sighed. 'Have I not been saying
this, Baby Randy?'

They were interrupted by the astrodog. It had
finished licking all the moisture off the cosmonaut's
suit. Now it produced a sound and smell that were
most unwelcome in the cramped confines (and
already stale air) of the International Space Station.[44]

'It's at times like this,' said Colonel Randy,
wrinkling up his nose, 'that I really wish we could
open the windows.'

33. Losing its fizz

The bagggoon landed in a paddock 50 kilometres
from the laboratory. Dr Hu phoned the CSIRO,
which sent a fleet of trucks, tankers and a big
mobile crane to meet them. A crew of specially
trained technicians pumped the precious ginger beer

---

[44] For more information, re-read Chapter 10.

carefully into the tankers, then the crane operator loaded the Voovl and the deflated bagggoon onto two large trucks. The whole convoy drove slowly back to Hakea Heights.

'The test flight was a resounding success,' Dr Hu told a press conference on the television news that evening. 'Everything ran like clockwork.'

'Does that mean you are now ready to repair the ozone layer?' a reporter asked.

'Almost ready,' said Dr Hu. 'First I have to replace the ginger beer we lost today.'

'How did you lose ginger beer, Doctor?' asked someone else. 'Did the bagggoon spring a leak?'

'No. I had to release some in order to return to earth,' explained the scientist. 'After every flight I have to top it up.'

'How long will it take to replace the ginger beer you lost today?' asked the reporter.

'I'll be working around the clock,' Dr Hu said, running a hand nervously through his hair. 'There isn't a lot of time.'

'Why the sense of urgency, Doctor?'

'Because my special ginger beer loses its fizz after four days,' he explained. 'And once it has lost its fizz, the bagggoon won't fly. So if I can't take off by Thursday, I'll have to ditch this entire batch of ginger beer and brew a new lot. Which will take six months. And in six months,' Dr Hu said, shaking his head, 'the ozone hole will be closed again. So it'll be another year before we can try again.'

There was silence as all the reporters thought about this. Finally one put up her hand.

'Doctor Hu,' she said, 'tell us about your passenger. Who is it? And how are they going to repair the ozone layer?'

'I'm afraid that's a secret,' Dr Hu said. 'And I'm sorry, ladies and gentlemen, but I don't have time for any more questions – I must get back to work.'

34. Peace and quokkas

Lukas switched off the television.

'Why is it a secret?' he squeaked. 'You could be famous, Astrid.'

'Not everyone wants to be famous, Lukas,' his big sister said.

'Brittany's right,' Astrid agreed. 'I don't want to be on TV. Already too many people know about me. Back home, people come to the door all the time asking me to fix things.'

Lukas rubbed his foot. 'But fixing things is good, Astrid.'

'Yeah, but not *all* the time. That's why it's so nice to be here. At last I can get a bit of peace and qu– 45'

'Hey, Super Glue,' said Kia-Jane, breezing into the room waving one hand in the air. 'Can you do your magic act for me? Look, I broke one of my nails.'

'You know I'm not allowed to fix people.'

'I'm not *people*, Supe, I'm your bestest buddy. Plus, you fixed your boyfriend.'

---

45 Quartz? Quinces? Quokkas? Your guess is ~~as good as~~ *better than* mine.

Astrid wondered whether it would be possible for a fixologist to murder someone. 'Show me,' she said wearily.

Kia-Jane plonked herself on the couch between Astrid and Lukas and dangled her left hand in Astrid's face. 'Disaster! My one perfect fingernail. I stop biting it for four whole weeks and *look what happens!*'

Astrid reached for the hand. 'I shouldn't be doing this.'

Lukas's big sister watched, fascinated, as the broken nail became whole again. 'My lips got all cracked and sunburned when I went horse riding the other day,' she said, moistening them with her tongue. 'Astrid, I wonder if you could . . . ?'

'I'm not *allowed* to fix people,' Astrid said. 'Something could go wrong.'

'What could go wrong?' asked Brittany.

'Well, there was this lady once and – '

'Super Glue, stop making excuses,' Kia-Jane interrupted. 'Fix her lips.'

'She doesn't want to,' rasped Lukas. 'Give her a break.'

'Give *me* a break,' said Brittany, rolling her eyes. 'I'm the one with cracked lips.'

'Something might go wrong,' Lukas squeaked.

'Something might go wrong with *you,* Foghorn, if you don't pull your head in!'

'It's okay,' said Astrid. She didn't want to cause a fight. 'Let's have a look at your lips, Brittany.'

35. Joined

'Mmmmm mmn mmmmn mmmn mmmnnn!' went Brittany.

'Darling, what is it?' asked her mother.

'She can't open her mouth,' rasped Lukas.

'It's my fault,' Astrid said.

'No, it isn't,' said Kia-Jane. 'It's my fault, Mrs Hu. I made Astrid do it.'

'Do what?' asked Mrs Hu.

'Fix Brittany's lips.'

Brittany's mother peered closely at her daughter's puckered-up mouth. 'What was wrong with your lips, darling?'

'Mmm mmmn mmmn mmmmmmn!'

'They were cracked,' Lukas translated.

'Mmmmmmn mnnnnnn!' went Brittany.

'Now they're stuck,' Lukas translated.

'Stuck?' said Mrs Hu.

'Together,' Kia-Jane explained. 'Her lips are stuck together.'

'Actually,' Astrid said, 'they're joined.'

36. Operation Ozone Fix

Next day, Mrs Hu took Brittany to hospital to have her lips separated.

Astrid felt terrible.

'It isn't your fault,' Kia-Jane and Lukas kept telling her. But she knew it was. Her parents had warned her a thousand times not to use her fixologist's skills on people. She should have known better.

Astrid, Kia-Jane and Lukas were helping Dr Hu prepare the bagggoon. All the ginger beer from the tankers had been pumped back into it overnight, but it still looked a bit limp and saggy. So they carried crate after crate of fresh ginger beer from a storeroom underneath the laboratory and emptied the bottles, one by one, into an upside-down funnel beneath the bagggoon. There were nearly 12,000 bottles. It was a painstaking job, because the full bottles flew away if you let go of them. So someone had to open the crate (upside down so the bottles wouldn't shoot up out of it) while someone else carefully removed a bottle. Another person would open the bottle (held upside down) with a bottle opener. Then the ginger beer could be emptied up into the funnel – very slowly so it wouldn't lose too much fizz.

It was a slow and repetitive job, but Astrid was glad to be busy. It took her mind off what had happened to Brittany.

Not for long. Kia-Jane kept making lip jokes.

'My *lips* are sealed,' she said when Astrid told her to stop referring to Lukas as her boyfriend.

'Don't give him any *lip*,' she said when Lukas growled at the galah for getting in their way.

'Oops,' she said when she nearly lost a bottle, 'it almost s-*lip*-ped out of my hand.'

It was nearly dark by the time Lukas placed the final empty bottle in its crate. The bagggoon towered above them, its clear plastic skin stretched taut as a drum.

'That's it,' Dr Hu announced, checking that the big, galah-proof chain holding the bagggoon to the gum tree was securely fastened. 'Barring unfavourable weather conditions, Operation Ozone Fix will commence tomorrow at first light.'

37. Impossible

The wind began at midnight. It was just a light breeze at first, gently rustling the curtains in the window of the Hus' spare bedroom. But half an hour later, when Astrid got up to close the window, it was howling.

'Kia-Jane, are you asleep?'

'No, I'm having a dream about this really tired and extremely gorgeous girl who's fast asleep, and then her friend, who doesn't like other people being asleep when she isn't, wakes the gorgeous girl by crashing the window closed and asking her if she's asleep.'

'Can you hear the wind?'

'That's a coincidence,' Kia-Jane said sleepily. 'In my dream, it's windy, too.'

'Kia-Jane, I'm serious,' said Astrid. 'If it's windy, the bagggoon mightn't be able to take off.'

'Don't worry, Supe, the wind will be gone by morning.'

Kia-Jane was wrong. The wind kept howling all night. Dr Hu looked extremely depressed at breakfast.

'Wouldn't you know, it's a southerly,' he said, looking out the window at the Voovl, bouncing and straining on the end of its chain as the wind tossed and buffeted the huge bagggoon. 'It would blow us *away* from the South Pole, rather than towards it.'

'But we have to try!' Astrid said. It was Thursday, their last chance to make it up to the ozone layer before the ginger beer lost its fizz.

Dr Hu shook his head. 'No, it's impossible. Operation Ozone Fix will have to wait another year.'

38. KA-REEEEEK!

Mrs Hu rang from the hospital to say that Brittany's operation had been a success. Since Operation Ozone Fix had been cancelled, Dr Hu decided to drive down to the city and pick them up. He left straight after breakfast, leaving Lukas and the two girls to do the housework.

'I can't believe he's just given up,' Astrid said as she unloaded the washing machine.

'You heard him,' squeaked Lukas, walking past carrying a mop and a bucket. 'The wind's blowing in the wrong direction.'

Kia-Jane plugged in the vacuum cleaner. 'Why don't you have a go at fixing the *weather*, Super Glue!'

Astrid carried the washing basket outside. How could Kia-Jane make jokes about it? The hole in the ozone layer was a serious problem. If they had to wait another year before it was fixed, thousands more people – even children! – could get skin cancer. Astrid began pegging the washing on the line, fighting the gusting southerly wind that threatened to tug each item of clothing out of her hands.

Chugga-bang-chugga-bang-chugga-bang-chugga-bang-chugga-bang!

What was that noise? Astrid turned around. Forty metres away, the huge bagggoon bounced and swayed and bucked in the wind. Also 40 metres away (but a bit lower down), the Voovl bounced and swayed and bucked and . . . shook. Yes, it was shaking! *Chugga-bang-chugga-bang-chugga-bang-chugga-bang-chugga-bang!*

Dropping a damp sock back into the washing basket, Astrid stared hard at the Voovl. Its passenger door was flapping open – that's what was making the banging noise. But the *chugga* noise was coming from the *top* of the Voovl.

Astrid ran back into the house and nearly slipped over on the freshly mopped kitchen floor. 'Lukas, someone's turned on the fizzifier!'

He dropped the mop and followed her outside.

'Maybe it came on by accident,' he squeaked, as they approached the tree where the bagggoon was chained. They stared up at the bouncing, bucking, swaying, shaking, *chugga-banging* Voovl.

'It might be Kia-Jane playing a joke.'

'No, she's vacuuming the lounge.' Lukas raised his voice. 'IS SOMEBODY IN THERE?' he shouted.

'I-I-IS SO-SO-SOMEBODY I-I-IN TH-TH-THERE?' somebody shouted back.

Astrid and Lukas looked at each other.

'The galah!' said Astrid.

'The galah!' said Lukas.

'Th-th-the ga-ga-galah!' said the galah.

'How did it get in there?' Lukas asked.

'The door must have come open in the wind,' said Astrid. She looked up at the Voovl, which was pulling and straining at the thick branch where Dr Hu had chained it. 'We'd better get the galah out of there and turn the fizzifier off before – 46'

'KA-REEEEEK!' the galah interrupted.

Stop press. On second thoughts, that might *not* have been the galah. Some big cracks had just –

'KA-KA-KA-REEEEEK!'

That was the galah. But as I was about to say, some big cracks had just appeared in the earth all around the base of the tree, and the ground seemed to be bulging upwards.

'Quick!' Astrid cried. 'We haven't got much time!'

She was right. Thirty seconds later, the bagggoon wrenched the tree right out of the ground and whisked it, roots and all, high into the sky.

---

46 Before lunch? Before the galah does? Before the end of the chapter? I guess we'll never know.

39. Countdown

But a lot of things can happen in thirty seconds. Here are some of them.

Inside the house, Kia-Jane had just made an interesting discovery. She had been vacuuming in the gap behind the couch when something quite large had gone *whoop-rattle-rattle-rattle* up the hose. Turning the machine off, Kia-Jane pulled the end off the vacuum cleaner and opened the dustbag. Inside she discovered a cute little electric-blue mobile phone.

'Lukas, whose is this?' she asked, walking through to the kitchen.

But Lukas wasn't in the kitchen. He was outside, and he was about to leave the planet.

'I'll turn the fizzifier off,' he squeaked, 27 seconds from lift-off.

A rope ladder dangled from the open door of the Voovl, reaching nearly all the way to the ground. Twenty-five seconds from lift-off, Lukas grabbed hold of it and began clambering up.

Twenty-four seconds from lift-off, Kia-Jane happened to glance out the kitchen window. What she saw caused her to forget all about the mobile phone, which she stuffed absent-mindedly into her pocket as she made for the door.

Twenty-one seconds from lift-off, Astrid saw a large crack appear at the base of the branch where the chain was secured.

Twenty seconds from lift-off, Kia-Jane came racing outside.

Nineteen seconds from lift-off, Astrid began climbing the tree to fix the cracked branch.

Eighteen seconds from lift-off, Kia-Jane called, 'Hey, Supe, what's going on?'

Fifteen seconds from lift-off, Astrid called over her shoulder, 'The stupid thing turned the fizzifier on!'

Thirteen seconds from lift-off (and four seconds from the tree), Kia-Jane asked, 'What stupid thing?'

Twelve seconds from lift-off, the galah said, 'Th-th-the ga-ga-galah!'

Eleven seconds from lift-off, Lukas began hauling himself in through the Voovl's passenger door.

Ten seconds from lift-off, Astrid reached the branch and began fixing the crack.

Nine seconds from lift-off, Kia-Jane reached the tree. 'Lukas,' she called, 'can you turn it off?'

Eight seconds from lift-off, and still half out of the car, Lukas said, 'I'm trying! Can you hold the ladder steady?'

Seven seconds from lift-off, something went, 'KA-REEEEEK!'

Six seconds from lift-off, something else went, 'KA-KA-KA-REEEEEK!'

Five seconds from lift-off, Lukas finally managed to struggle into the Voovl and the door banged shut behind him.

Four seconds from lift-off, Kia-Jane said, 'Hey, the ground's moving!'

Three seconds from lift-off, Astrid said, 'Hey, the tree's moving!'

Two seconds from lift-off, Lukas reached for the lever to turn the fizzifier off.

One second from lift-off, the galah, which was sitting on the lever, pecked his finger.

Zero seconds from lift-off . . . well, they lifted off, of course.

40. Aaaaaaaaaaaargh! x 5

'Aaaaaaaaaaaargh!' rasped Lukas, shaking his sore finger.

'Aaaaaaaaaaaargh!' shrieked Astrid, legs and arms wrapped tightly around her branch as the ground dropped away below her.

'Aaaaaaaaaaaargh!' squealed Kia-Jane, holding on desperately to the rope ladder as she was whisked up into the sky.

'Aaaaaaaaaaaargh!' cried the captain of Qantas Flight 99 from Hobart, banking sharply to avoid what looked like a Volvo and a thirty-metre gum tree dangling out of a cloud directly in front of his 767.

'Aaaaaaaaaaaargh!' squawked the galah, bobbing its head up and down and doing a little victory dance on the fizzifier lever.

41. Lu-Lu-Lukas's pro-pro-problem

Kia-Jane was the first to recover (well, she was second, if you count the galah).

'Hey, Supe!' she called across from the dangling rope ladder. 'Don't look down!'

'Don't look down, yourself!' Astrid called back from the dangling gum tree.

Then they both *did* look down, which was a mistake because they were very high. And getting higher every second. Above them, they could hear the *chugga-chugga-chugga-chugga-chugga* of the fizzifier.

'I thought Lukas was going to turn that thing off,' Kia-Jane said.

'Something must have gone wrong. Can you climb up and see?'

Kia-Jane struggled her way up the rope ladder and banged on the door.

It clicked open about five centimetres and Lukas peered down through the gap. 'K-K-Kia-Jane! Wh-wh-what o-o-on e-e-earth a-a-are y-y-you do-do-doing he-he-here?'

'Not on earth,' she said, 'in sky. Aren't you going to invite me in?'

Lukas pushed the door wide open and helped her into the shaking, bumping Voovl.

'W-w-weren't y-y-you g-g-going t-t-to tur-tur-turn th-th-the fi-fi-fizzifier o-o-off?' Kia-Jane asked.

'B-b-be m-m-my g-g-guest,' said Lukas.

Kia-Jane reached for the lever and the galah pecked her.

'Ou-ou-ouch!'

'Ou-ou-ouch!' went the galah.

'Y-y-you s-s-see m-m-my pro-pro-problem,' squeaked Lukas.

'I-i-is th-th-there an-an-another w-w-way o-o-of g-g-getting d-d-down?' Kia-Jane asked, eyeing the galah warily. (It had a very large, very sharp beak.)

'W-w-we c-c-could b-b-bleed o-o-off s-s-some gin-gin-ginger b-b-beer.'

'H-h-how d-d-do w-w-we d-d-do th-th-that?'

'I-I-I'm n-n-not s-s-sure,' Lukas rasped, waving his hand at two identical brass taps on the dashboard. 'Th-th-the co-co-controls are d-d-different fro-fro-from th-th-the Ho-Ho-Holden. I-i-it's a sh-sh-shame A-A-Astrid's n-n-not h-h-here; sh-sh-she m-m-might kn-kn-know wh-wh-which I-i-is th-th-the ri-ri-right one.'

Kia-Jane raised her eyebrows. 'H-h-have I-I-I g-g-got a sur-sur-surprise f-f-for y-y-you!'

42. Don't!

Leaning out of the Voovl, with Kia-Jane holding on to his belt for safety, Lukas swayed the rope ladder back and forth like a giant pendulum until Astrid was able to catch hold of it. She swung out of the tree and climbed up into the car.

'Wh-wh-what a p-p-pong!' said Lukas. 'A-A-Astrid, y-y-you s-s-smell li-li-like a gu-gu-gum t-t-tree!'

Lukas had a lot to learn when it came to talking to girls, but he did have a point – Astrid smelt like a gum tree. The galah noticed it too.

'Gu-gu-gum t-t-tree!' it said, and flapped across to her shoulder.[47]

Lukas immediately grabbed the fizzifier lever and turned it off.

'Phew, that's a relief,' said everyone except the galah.

'Phew, that's a relief.' (Okay, *that* was the galah. But the other three said it first.)

Dr Hu's modifications had turned the Voovl into a two-seater, so there wasn't a lot of room. Astrid and Kia-Jane shared the passenger seat, while Lukas

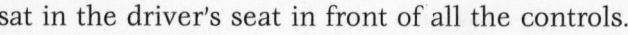

sat in the driver's seat in front of all the controls.

'It's getting a bit cold,' he squeaked. 'Do you know how to turn the heaters on, Astrid?'

'Press that red button next to your left knee.'

Lukas activated the interior hair-dryers. 'So how do I get us home?' he asked.

Astrid showed him the switch for the exterior hair-dryers. 'That's the jet propulsion system. And you steer with the little joystick.'

'Um, how do I know which way to go?'

'Use the compass,' Astrid said. 'Which way are we heading?'

'South.'

[47] Galahs like gum trees, in case you didn't know.

'That's impossible. The wind's coming from the south. We should be going north.'

'Take a look for yourself,' rasped Lukas.

Astrid leaned sideways to read the compass. 'The useless thing must be broken,' she said.

'Well, fix it, Super Glue,' said Kia-Jane.

Astrid touched the compass with the tips of her fixologist's fingers but the reading still showed south. 'I don't get it,' she muttered.

'Maybe the wind changed,' squeaked Lukas.

'I think I know what's happened,' Kia-Jane said. 'How high are we?'

Lukas consulted the altimeter. '10,600 metres.'

'That probably explains it. I read once that when you're really high up, the wind sometimes blows in the opposite direction to the wind lower down.'

'So we really are heading south,' Astrid said thoughtfully.

'Looks like it,' Kia-Jane agreed. 'Lukas, you'd better get this flying circus turned around before we end up in Tasmania.'

But Lukas wasn't listening. He was frowning at the altimeter gauge. 'Hey, this thing isn't working, either. It says we're now 11,300 metres above sea level. And still climbing.'

Kia-Jane gave Astrid a nudge in the ribs. 'Do your magic, Supe.'

'I don't need to,' Astrid said excitedly. 'We *are* still climbing. Can't you feel it?'

There was a moment's silence. They all felt the upwards movement.

'It doesn't make sense,' rasped Lukas. 'I turned the fizzifier off ages ago.'

Astrid nodded. (And so did the galah on her shoulder.) 'But it was running for nearly half an hour *before* you turned it off, Lukas. So the ginger beer must be mega-fizzy by now.'

'I'd better jettison some, then,' Lukas squeaked, reaching for one of the big brass taps mounted in the middle of the dashboard.

'Don't!' said Astrid. 'That's the oxygen one.'

Lukas grabbed the other tap.

'Don't!' said Astrid. 'I've got an idea.'

43. Heroes

Kia-Jane and Lukas both stared at her as if she were mad. She had just told them her plan.

'No way!' said Kia-Jane.

'No way!' squeaked Lukas.

'No way!' squawked the galah.

Astrid shook her head. 'I can't believe you guys. We could be heroes!'

'We're just kids,' rasped Lukas. 'We don't even know how to fly this thing.'

'It's flying, isn't it?'

'Yes, but it's totally out of control.'

'*And* there's an entire gum tree hanging from the tow bar,' Kia-Jane pointed out.

'The gum tree doesn't seem to be a problem,' said Astrid. 'You never know, it might even come in handy later on.'

Kia-Jane laughed. 'For firewood, I suppose?'

'Maybe,' Astrid said seriously. 'Or to float on.'

'To *float* on?'

'Well, who knows where we'll land.'

'That's it!' Lukas squeaked. 'I'm taking us down.'

He grabbed hold of the ginger beer tap, but Astrid clutched his arm before he could turn it.

'Think of your father, Lukas. Think of the thousands of hours' work he's put into this project. If you turn that tap, it'll all be for nothing.'

'It won't be for nothing,' Lukas rasped. 'At least now he knows the bagggoon actually works. He can make another attempt to fix the ozone hole next year.'

'Millions more people could contract skin cancer by next year.'

Lukas's fingers reluctantly released their grip on the tap. He sat back in his seat with a loud sigh. 'Okay, Astrid, you win. Let's be heroes.'

'Wait a minute! Wait a minute!' said Kia-Jane. 'Don't I get a vote?'

'Well, I suppose so,' said Astrid. She looked at Lukas, who shrugged his shoulders.

'It's all in or none in, I guess.'

'Good,' said Kia-Jane. 'In that case . . . ' she paused dramatically '. . . I want to be a hero too.'

'Hero! Hero! Hero!' squawked the galah.

'That makes it unanimous,' said Astrid.

44. Bu-bu-bummer

Three hours later, Astrid was peering through the ozonescope. They were halfway to the South Pole and almost underneath the hole in the ozone layer. Through Dr Hu's clever invention the hole looked like a massive blue circle, high above them, surrounded by bright orange sky.

'What's our current altitude, Lukas?'

'15,278 metres,' he squeaked.

'That can't be right,' Kia-Jane said. 'We reached 15,000 metres half an hour ago.'

'I know,' rasped Lukas. 'The ginger beer must be running out of fizz.'

'Bummer,' said Astrid.

'Bummer,' said Kia-Jane.

'Bummer,' squeaked Lukas, and pulled the lever to activate the fizzifier.

'Bu-bu-bummer,' squawked the galah.

45. Dr Hu, where are you?

With the help of the fizzifier, the bagggoon soon began to climb once more.

At 16,808 metres, Kia-Jane said, 'H-h-how hi-hi-high i-i-is th-th-the o-o-ozone la-la-layer, Lu-Lu-Lukas?'

At 17,825 metres, Lukas squeaked, 'I-i-it s-s-starts a-a-at a-a-around 19-19-19,000 m-m-metres.'

At 18,164 metres, Kia-Jane said, 'H-h-how a-a-are y-y-you go-go-going t-t-to fi-fi-fix i-i-it, Su-Su-Supe?'

At 18,313 metres, Astrid said, 'Wh-wh-what d-d-do y-y-you me-me-mean?'

At 18,406 metres, Kia-Jane said, 'W-w-well, a-a-are y-y-you go-go-going t-t-to sta-sta-stand o-o-on th-th-the Voo-Voo-Voovl's r-r-roof, o-o-or ha-ha-hang ou-ou-out th-th-the d-d-door, o-o-or wha-wha-what?'

At 18,524 metres, Astrid frowned.

At 18,727 metres, Astrid looked worried.

At 19,041 metres, Astrid said, 'U-u-um . . .'

At 19,229 metres, Astrid said, 'I-I-I d-d-don't kn-kn-know.'

At 19,263 metres, Kia-Jane, Lukas and the galah said (and rasped), 'Y-y-you d-d-don't kn-kn-know!!!?'

At 19,290 metres, Lukas turned the fizzifier off (thank goodness for that!) and rasped, 'What do you mean, you don't know?'

From 19,295 metres to 19,411 metres, Astrid looked embarrassed.

At 19,433 metres, Lukas squeaked, 'Well?'

At 19,501 metres, Astrid said, 'We didn't discuss it, actually. I guess your dad was going to explain it when the time came.'

At 19,623 metres, Lukas rasped, 'Well, the time *has* come.'

At 19,664 metres, Astrid said, 'I just *don't know*! If I open the door we'll all freeze to death. Plus, we'll lose all our oxygen.'

At 19,732 metres, Lukas squeaked, 'He must have a plan.'

At 19,909 metres, Astrid said, 'But we don't know what it is.'

At 20,264 metres, Kia-Jane said, 'Dr Hu, where are you when we need you?'

46. Don't just sit there . . .

At 21,500 metres, Astrid said, 'Kia-Jane, you've got really bony hips!'

'That isn't my hip,' Kia-Jane said indignantly. 'There's something in my pocket.'

They were squashed really close together in the Voovl's passenger seat. Kia-Jane had to squirm sideways and squeeze her hand down to get to her hip pocket. Out came a tiny blue mobile phone.

'Hey, I forgot all about this.' She held it up. 'Look familiar, Lukas?'

'It's Brittany's.' Lukas reached for the phone. 'She's always losing it.'

'Is the battery charged?' asked Astrid.

Lukas switched the phone on. 'Looks like it.' Both girls stared at him.

'What?' squeaked Lukas.

'Don't just sit there . . . ,' said Astrid.

'Use it,' Kia-Jane finished for her.

47. Athhrid Thhpark, thhikkthologithhhht

Dr Hu stood still for a few moments, puzzling over a large hole in the lawn.

'Joanna,' he said, wandering inside carrying two suitcases, 'someone has taken our tree.'

Mrs Hu was standing in the middle of the kitchen with a mop in her hand and a frown on her face. 'What tree, Augustus?'

'The one the bagggoon was chained to.'

'Is it all right?'

'It's gone.'

'I meant the bagggoon.'

Dr Hu put down one of the suitcases and scratched his head. 'Oh, dear,' he said.

Brittany walked out of her bedroom. She had 67 stitches in her lips but at least they were no longer joined.

'Hath anyone theen my thone?'

'Your what?' asked her mother.

'My thone.'

'Your throne?'

'My thone.'

They were interrupted by a loud ringing sound. Brittany pointed excitedly. *'Thone! Thone!'*

'I'm sorry, darling,' her mother said, 'I can't hear you because of the phone.'

Rolling her eyes, Brittany picked up the receiver. 'Yethh?'

Then she held it out to her father. 'Ith Athhrid Thhpark. Thhee wanthh t' know how t' thhikkth th'othone layer.'

48. Now we're in business

Dr Hu told Astrid to pull the 'bonnet release' lever.

'Where's that?' she said.

'Who's in the driver's seat?' asked the scientist.

'Lukas.'

'May I speak to him, please.'

Following his father's directions, Lukas released the bonnet. Instead of popping up like a normal car bonnet, it folded back like a convertible's roof. Then, very slowly, a large see-through dome rose out of the engine compartment. Protruding from the dome were two pink rubber gloves. By crawling through a little trapdoor under the dashboard, Astrid was able to climb inside the dome and poke her fingers into the gloves and out into the damaged ozone surrounding the car.

'Good old Dad! He's thought of everything,' Lukas squeaked admiringly, covering the phone's mouthpiece so Dr Hu wouldn't hear and get a swollen head.

'Not quite everything,' Astrid called back,

waggling the gloves at Lukas and Kia-Jane, who were watching her through the windscreen. 'I can't fix anything like this.'

'Why not, Super Glue?'

'My fingers have to actually *touch* something to fix it. There's a layer of rubber between them and the ozone.'

'Back to the drawing board, Dad,' Lukas rasped into the phone.

'Wait a minute,' said Astrid. 'I've got an idea. Has anyone got a pin?'

Nobody had a pin, but Kia-Jane found a piece of sharp wire in the glove box. Astrid used it to poke tiny holes in all ten of the rubber gloves' fingers.

'Now my fingertips will have direct contact with the ozone,' she said.

But as soon as she stuck her hands back into the gloves and began thinking fixing thoughts, her amazing fixologist's fingers fixed the holes instead of the ozone!

'Back to the drawing-board, Dad!' rasped the galah.

So much had been going on that Astrid had forgotten about the galah. It was still perched on her shoulder, its razor-sharp beak just millimetres from her cheek.

'Can you do me a favour?' she asked it, turning the gloves inside out so they poked into the dome instead of out of it. 'Bite the ends off these fingers.'

Crunch!

'Yeeeeeeeeeeeeeeow!' screeched Astrid.

The galah had bitten the end off a finger, all right, but not one of the glove's fingers.

'Someone get me a bandaid!'

'You don't need a bandaid,' Kia-Jane said. 'You need a fixologist.'

'I'm not allowed to fix people,' said Astrid. And anyway, she couldn't fix herself. (She'd tried lots of times, but it never worked.)

There was a first-aid kit under the driver's seat. Lukas carefully bound up Astrid's finger. He was very gentle.

'There you go,' he squeaked, snipping the end off the plaster with a small pair of scissors. 'Good as new.'

It wasn't as good as new, of course. Now Astrid only had nine uncovered fingers to fix the ozone layer. But nine was enough. Or it should have been.

'Give me those scissors, Lukas.'

Astrid snipped the ends off all the gloves' fingers. As soon as she did, air from the pressurised Voovl began hissing out into the low-pressure atmosphere outside and pushed the gloves right-way-out. Dropping the scissors, Astrid stuffed her

 hands into the gloves, plugging the holes (but not fixing them this time because the snipped-off ends were still on the floor beneath her knees and couldn't be rejoined).

'Now we're in business,' she said, wriggling the bare tips of her fingers in the ozone layer outside the dome.

49. Blue waves

'Nothing's happening!' said Kia-Jane.

'You can't see it with the naked eye,' Astrid said, screwing up her face in pain – it was *freezing* out there. 'Use the ozonescope.'

Kia-Jane looked through the scope. 'Cool!'

'You can say that again,' said Astrid.

'Cool!' said the galah.

'Give me a look, Kia-Jane,' rasped Lukas. He put his eye to the ozonescope. 'Wicked!'

'What's happening?' asked his father, still on the mobile phone.

'Astrid's fixing the ozone.'

'Tell me what you can see, Lukas.'

'Dad, it's totally awesome! There are all these blue waves around Astrid's fingers. They're shooting off into the sky like humungous ripples.'

'Blue waves?' his father said slowly. 'Are you sure they're blue?'

'Blue as, um, roses.'

'Roses aren't blue.'

'Well, blue ones are.'

Dr Hu was silent for a few moments. 'They should be orange.'

'Blue roses should be orange?'

'No. The waves coming from Astrid's fingers should be orange.'

Lukas shook his head. 'The orange is further away, Dad. Astrid's blue waves are pushing it back.'

'Galloping gastropods!'[48] gasped Dr Hu. 'Tell her to stop!'

'Stop?' squeaked Lukas. 'But it's working really well, Dad. You should see the blue waves. They look really – '

'It's working in reverse,' his father interrupted. 'Instead of repairing the ozone, she's destroying it. MAKE HER STOP!'

Lukas lowered the mobile. 'Astrid, Dad says you've got to stop.'

'Stop?' she said, gritting her teeth against the terrible cold. The outside of the dome (and her fingers) was covered in ice crystals. 'Is it fixed already? Have I fixed the ozone layer?'

'No. He says it's working in reverse! You're destroying it, not fixing – '

'STOP!' the galah screeched in Astrid's ear.

She didn't need to be told twice. In fact, the second time had nearly deafened her. Ears ringing, Astrid dragged her frozen hands back inside the dome.

Immediately, the ringing sound was replaced by a loud *hisssssssssssssssssssssssssssssss*!

'You'd better fix those gloves, Supe,' Kia-Jane said. 'We're losing pressure in here.'

Without Astrid's fingers to plug them up, the

48 Really fast snails.

gloves were letting oxygen out into the atmosphere at an alarming rate. Already it was becoming difficult to breathe inside the Voovl. And cold.

Astrid scrabbled round on the floor for the snipped-off ends of the gloves. She found one and tried to repair one of the glove-fingers with it. But her own fingers were icy and numb, and even though she was thinking fixing thoughts, the molecules wouldn't join properly. Suddenly – *Floop!* – the escaping air shot the tiny scrap of rubber out into the sky.

She tried another one and the same thing happened.

'I can't do it!' she gasped.

'You've got to,' cried Kia-Jane. 'We'll run out of oxygen!'

Astrid tried three more times, and lost three more glove-tips.

'It's impossible!'

'Astrid, come back into the car,' Lukas gasped. His voice had become even more squeaky and raspy than usual. 'I'll retract the dome.'

As soon as she had scrambled back into the Voovl, Lukas pushed the bonnet release lever back to the closed position. Nothing happened. He grabbed the phone.

'Dad, how do we retract the dome?'

'It doesn't retract,' Dr Hu said. He sounded very faint. 'Once it's open, it stays . . .'

There was silence.

'Dad?' Lukas wheezed. 'Dad, Dad? Dad . . . ?' He looked at the girls, his face as white as a rose.[49] 'The battery's gone flat.'

'Did he say anything about the dome?' Astrid asked, hugging her stinging, frozen hands under her windcheater for warmth.

'Only . . .' Lukas took a big, wheezy breath, 'only that it . . . *wheeze* . . . doesn't retract.'

The three of them gazed out at the gloves. The pressurised air whooshing into the atmosphere had blown up the gloves to the size of cows' udders. It was becoming hard to breathe inside the Voovl, and it was growing colder by the second.

'Tap!' Kia-Jane said suddenly.

The other two gaped at her, their mouths blowing clouds of white condensation into the chill, oxygen-starved air around them.

Kia-Jane pointed at the dashboard. 'The tap, Lukas! Release some ginger beer.'

Finally he understood. Leaning forward, his breath sawing and whistling as if he'd just run a marathon, Lukas opened the ginger-beer tap as far as it would go.

50. Astrid Spark, lifesaver

From above them came the bubbling noise of escaping ginger beer. But it wasn't nearly as loud as the hiss of escaping oxygen.

49 A white one.

They watched the altimeter: 23,458 metres, 23,457 metres, 23,456 metres . . .

At 23,452 metres, Kia-Jane said, 'So . . . slow.'

At 23,245 metres, Astrid groaned, 'Really . . . slow.'

At 23,188 metres, Lukas wheezed, 'Too . . . *wheeze* . . . slow.'

At 23,163 metres, all three of them were feeling fuzzy-headed and sleepy. The hissing seemed even louder, and the gloves had swollen to the size of beach balls.

At 23,094 metres, Kia-Jane said, 'Any moment now . . . and they're going to . . . burst.'

At 22,859 metres, Lukas wheezed, 'If . . . *wheeze* . . . they burst . . . *wheeze* . . . it's . . . all over . . . *wheeze* . . . red rover!'

At 22,667 metres, Astrid whispered, 'They won't . . . burst.'

At 22,632 metres, Kia-Jane said, 'Wanna . . . bet?'

At 22,525 metres, Kia-Jane said, 'Well . . .? Do . . . you . . . wanna . . . bet?'

At 22,110, Kia-Jane turned to see why Astrid wasn't answering her.

At 21,869 metres, Kia-Jane whispered, 'Now . . . where . . . did . . . Supe . . . get . . . to?'

At 21,494 metres, Lukas pointed. 'There . . . *wheeze* . . . she . . . is.'

He was right. There she was, inside the dome, with both hands stuck up into the gloves, her fingers plugging the holes.

And the hissing had stopped.

'Astrid . . . Spark,' gasped Kia-Jane, 'you're . . . a . . . lifesaver!'

51. GOING TO CRASH!

'Lukas, you'd better turn the tap off,' Kia-Jane said.

They were in heavy cloud. There was nothing to see through the icy windscreen apart from the vague, grey shape of Astrid sticking her blue-tipped fingers out of the frosty white dome. The altimeter showed 4,200 metres. It was easier to breathe now, and the interior hair-dryers had replaced some of the warmth they'd lost.

'Lukas, I think you'd better turn the tap off,' Kia-Jane repeated at 3,984 metres.

He ignored her.

'Lukas,' Kia-Jane said at 3,441 metres, 'we're low enough now. I think we should stop our descent and try to work out where we are.'

Still he ignored her.

'LUKAS!' Kia-Jane yelled at 2,109 metres. 'WE'RE GOING TO CRASH! WHAT'S THE MATTER WITH YOU?'

She shook Lukas's arm, and his head flopped forward onto his chest. Kia-Jane screamed.

'What's going on?' Astrid called from the dome.

'It's Lukas. I think he's dead!'

Astrid dragged her frozen hands out of the gloves and scrambled back into the Voovl. She bent over Lukas, released his seat belt and gently lifted his head back. His face was completely white and his eyes were closed. 'He isn't dead,' she said after a few moments. 'Listen, he's still breathing.'

They could both hear it now, a faint wheezy echo from deep inside his chest.

'What's wrong with him?' Kia-Jane asked.

'He's having an asthma attack. Lukas, can you hear me?'

His eyelids fluttered open, but his eyes seemed glazed and unfocused.

'Lukas, where's your inhaler?'

His lips moved but no sound came out.

'I'm going to go through your pockets,' Astrid told him gently.

He managed a tiny shake of his head. 'Left it . . . *wheeze* . . . home.'

'This is definitely not good,' Kia-Jane muttered.

Astrid tilted Lukas's seat as far back as it would go. 'We have to make him comfortable,' she said. 'Then we'll take the bagggoon down to 1,000 metres where it's warmer and there's more oxygen . . . '

Suddenly Kia-Jane remembered why she had tried to get Lukas's attention in the first place. 'We *are* down to 1,000 metres!' she cried, pointing at the plunging altimeter reading. 'Quick, turn the ginger beer tap off!'

Astrid wound the tap fully closed, then both girls anxiously watched the altimeter.

868 metres, 836 metres, 799 metres . . .

'It isn't slowing,' whispered Kia-Jane.

'We've lost too much ginger beer,' whispered Astrid. 'We're – '

'GOING TO CRASH!' shrieked the galah.

52. The Voovl has landed

Astrid felt a light touch on her arm. Lukas was trying to tell her something. She leaned close to him.

'Fizz . . . fier,' he wheezed.

Of course! Astrid grabbed the fizzifier lever and swung it to the 'on' position.

Chugga-chugga-chugga-chugga-chugga!

There was nothing to see through the windscreen, which was completely iced over now. All they could do was watch the altimeter. And hope.

434 metres, 406 metres, 372 metres . . .

'W-w-we're st-st-still f-f-falling,' said Kia-Jane.

'Bu-bu-but w-w-we're slo-slo-slowing,' said Astrid.

201 metres, 182 metres, 147 metres . . .

'I-I-I wi-wi-wish w-w-we c-c-could s-s-see ou-ou-out!' said Kia-Jane.

The windscreen was a white sheet of ice. It didn't make sense. They were down to 100 metres and it seemed to be getting colder, not warmer.

77 metres, 58 metres, 44 metres . . .

'B-b-brace y-y-yourse-se-selves!' said Astrid.

'B-b-brace y-y-yourse-se-selves!' said the galah.

Crunch!

Then there was complete silence (except for Lukas's wheezing breath). Even the fizzifier had stopped.

Kia-Jane cleared her throat. 'Ladies and gentlemen,' she announced, 'the Voovl has landed.'

53. The South Gum Tree

Kia-Jane's door was jammed. Astrid leaned carefully across Lukas and tried the one on his side. It creaked open.

Directly below her was a black-and-white penguin.

'Hullo,' Astrid said. 'What are you doing here?'

'Kraaaaaaak!'[50] said the penguin.

'I live here, plankton-brain!'[51] said the galah.

There were more black-and-white penguins in the distance, a big circle of them – they looked like Collingwood supporters crowded around the boundary of a football oval. Only football ovals aren't white.

'I think we're at the zoo,' Kia-Jane whispered, peering out over Astrid's shoulder.

'It's too cold for the zoo,' said Astrid. 'And too icy. I think it's the South Pole.'

'*The South Pole?!!!*' said Kia-Jane.

'*The South Pole?!!!*' said the galah.

'*Kraaaaaaak?!!!*'[52] said the penguin.

---

50 Penguin-speak for: 'I live here, plankton-brain!'
51 Galah-speak for: 'Kraaaaaaak!'
52 Penguin-speak for: '*I live here, plankton-brain?!!!*' (Penguins have an extremely limited vocabulary.)

'In fact,' Astrid said, craning her neck to look down, 'we seem to be *on* the South Pole.' She was wrong. It was the South Gum Tree. And the Voovl was stuck in its topmost branches.

54. Bye bye bagggoon

Astrid lowered the rope ladder, then she and Kia-Jane climbed down to explore. They closed the door after them so Lukas would stay warm.

'I'm really worried about him,' Astrid said when they reached the ground.

'I'm worried about *all* of us,' said Kia-Jane, bending to examine how their not-very-gentle landing had embedded the gum tree's roots in the ice. 'How did we get to Antarctica?'

'That upper-atmosphere wind must have been stronger than we thought.'

They soon discovered they weren't in Antarctica. They were on an iceberg, surrounded by ocean. There were more icebergs in the distance, but theirs was the only one with a gum tree.

'At least we've got shade,' Kia-Jane said.

In fact, they had too much shade. The bagggoon was still attached to the Voovl. With half its ginger beer gone, the enormous plastic bag flopped and billowed in the sky above them, casting the whole iceberg into shadow. They needed sunshine to work the Voovl's solar-powered hair-dryer heaters.

'We've got to get rid of the bagggoon,' Astrid said. 'There's not enough ginger beer left to lift us off anyway.'

The bagggoon was attached to the Voovl by four nylon cables. These were fastened to spring-loaded clips on the front and rear bumpers of the car. Astrid and Kia-Jane climbed back up the tree and undid the clips. It was difficult for Astrid because her fingers were still half frozen from plugging up the gloves and she'd lost all feeling in them. But finally the bagggoon was released. The swirling ocean wind ripped it free of the hose attaching it to the fizzifier and off it flew, ginger beer spraying in all directions.

Sitting on the Voovl, at the top of a gum tree, on an iceberg, in the middle of the Southern Ocean, the girls watched the bagggoon until it was just a tiny speck in the sky.[53]

---

[53] Author's note: In less dire circumstances, and had there been a recycle-bin handy, our two heroines would undoubtedly have disposed of the bagggoon in a more caring and environmentally friendly manner.

'Well,' Kia-Jane said sadly, 'now we really *are* on our own.'

'Kraaaaaaak!' said 800 black-and-white penguins (and one pink-and-grey one).

There was also one very large elephant seal lying on the edge of the ice, but it didn't say anything.

55. Not working

'Where . . . *wheeze* . . . are we?' wheezed Lukas.

Astrid and Kia-Jane had just scrambled back inside the Voovl.

'You're never going to believe it,' Kia-Jane said.

'On an iceberg,' Astrid told him.

Lukas rolled his eyes towards Astrid – he was too weak to move his head. 'Ice . . . *wheeze* . . . berg?'

'Sssssssh. Try not to talk,' she said gently. He looked really bad. 'I'll get us out of here, Lukas.'

Kia-Jane caught her eye. 'How?' she mouthed.

Astrid was fumbling to get the back off the mobile phone. 'I'm going to fix this.'

'It's not broken. The battery's just gone flat.'

'I'm a fixologist,' Astrid boasted. 'I can fix flat batteries in my sleep!'

She was wrong. (She was also awake.) When she removed the plastic cover and rubbed her numb fingers all over the battery, the display stayed dead.

Lukas took a long, squeaky breath. 'Astrid . . . *wheeze* . . . is something . . . *wheeze* . . . wrong?'

'My fingers,' she whispered, two large tears running down her cheeks, 'they're not working!'

56. Wrecked!

It was Kia-Jane who worked it out. Astrid's fingers had nearly frozen solid when she'd stuck them out of the dome during the bagggoon's descent. Somehow the extreme cold must have taken away their magnetic ability to fix things.

'They'll probably get better,' Kia-Jane said. 'You'll just have to warm them up a bit.'

For twenty minutes Astrid warmed her fingers in front of a hair-dryer, then she tried once more to fix the phone. Still it didn't work.

'They're wrecked!' she groaned, staring at her fingers in shocked disbelief. All her life she'd been a fixologist and now, just when it had become a matter of life and death, she had lost her special powers. 'I can't fix things any more!'

'Ass . . . *wheeze* . . . trid.'

Lukas was trying to say something. Astrid wiped the tears from her eyes and bent closer to him. 'What is it, Lukas?'

'Band . . . *wheeze* . . . aid.'

'You need a bandaid?'

He moved his eyes from side to side. 'Your . . . *wheeze* . . . '

Astrid waited, holding her breath, while Lukas struggled to get the next word out.

'. . . fin . . . *wheeze* . . . ger.'

'Lukas, you're a genius!' Kia-Jane cried. She grabbed hold of Astrid's left hand and isolated one of the fingers. 'Bandaid. Finger. The bandaid on *your* finger, Supe!'

Suddenly Astrid understood. She had been wearing a bandaid ever since the galah pecked her, which happened *before* she'd stuck her fingers out through the gloves. So the finger with the bandaid on it would have been protected from the full brunt of the chill. Quickly she peeled off the dressing. Underneath, her skin looked soft and white. The cut was quite deep, but the fingertip wasn't numb like the others. Biting her tongue, almost too nervous to try it, Astrid rubbed the battery with her freshly unwrapped finger.

57. Warm Barry

'It's no good,' Astrid said, tears of frustration in her eyes. 'I guess I'm no longer a fixologist.'

Kia-Jane pretended it didn't matter. 'They'll send planes and ships out looking for us.'

'But they won't know where to look,' Astrid said. 'They might even think we're still up in the sky. We've *got* to make contact with the outside world.'

'How?' asked Kia-Jane.

'Warm . . .' wheezed Lukas. His voice was very faint. Astrid bent close to him.

'What is it, Lukas?'

'Warm . . . bah . . . ree.'

Warm bah ree? Warm Barry? Warm . . . ?
Suddenly Astrid got it. Warm the battery! Kia-Jane
was right – Lukas *was* a genius. By heating a flat
battery, you could charge it up a bit. Removing the
little square battery from the mobile phone, Astrid
held it in front of a hair-dryer.

Twenty minutes later she had the phone
working. There was only enough charge to make
one call. Astrid wanted to phone Dr Hu, but she
didn't know his number, and Lukas was too weak
to tell her, so she called home.

Her mother answered on the first ring.

'Mum, it's Astrid.'

'Astrid!' Jacqui cried. Her voice sounded
extremely faint and it kept breaking up. 'Thank . . .
eavens you're . . . ight! We all . . . you . . . lost – '

'Mum, listen!' Astrid interrupted her, speaking
loudly and fast. 'The battery's running out, there
isn't much time. We're stuck on an iceberg and
Lukas is having an asthma attack. I don't know
where we are but it's somewhere down near
Antarctica. There are lots of other icebergs and it's
really cold and there are all these penguins and a
seal and the Voovl's stuck at the top of a gum tree
and we had to let go the bagggoon and Lukas hasn't
got his puffer and his lips are blue and Kia-Jane
and I are really . . . Mum? Are you still there,
Mum?'

The phone was dead.

'Is she going to send help?' Kia-Jane asked
anxiously.

'I don't know,' said Astrid. 'I'm not sure if she
heard anything I said.'

58. No longer a fixologist

They tried heating the battery again but this time it
didn't work. Then all the hair-dryers began to lose
power. Finally they stopped altogether.
Astrid glanced out the windscreen.

'The sun's going down, so the
solar panels have stopped working.'

She and Kia-Jane nearly froze
during the night. There were two
space blankets in the emergency pack
under the front seat, but the girls wrapped both of
them around Lukas. He was shaking uncontrollably,
his lips were blue[54] and he kept slipping in and out
of consciousness. His breath was laboured and
wheezy and irregular. It was horrible to listen to.
Astrid and Kia-Jane stayed awake, blowing on their
hands, talking, and cuddling together for warmth.
Luckily, because they were so close to the Antarctic,
the night didn't last very long. Within a few hours of
setting, the sun rose again.

'They'd better find us today,' Astrid murmured,
warming her hands in front of a hair-dryer as it
slowly hummed into action. 'I don't ever want to
live through another night like that.'

[54] As blue roses.

'Nor me,' said Kia-Jane.

Neither of them said it, but they both thought that Lukas *wouldn't* live through another night like that. He looked much worse than he had the day before. Not just his lips, but his whole face was bluish-white now. And, despite the cold, his skin was damp and clammy. He seemed to be unconscious. But they knew he was alive because of his rattly, wheezing breath.

'There must be something we can do,' Astrid said, with tears in her eyes.

'There is,' said Kia-Jane. 'He needs a drink.'

Among the supplies in the emergency pack they found a small gas stove and a billy. Astrid warmed some soup but they couldn't wake Lukas to drink any. Finally she and Kia-Jane had the soup themselves and shared a muesli bar and a block of chocolate.

'If my fingers still worked,' Astrid said, licking a speck of chocolate off her lips, 'I reckon I'd be able to do something for him.'

'Remember what you did to his sister,' Kia-Jane reminded her. 'You might make him *worse*!'

Astrid watched the whistly rise and fall of Lukas's chest under the space blankets. Kia-Jane was right. Astrid really had no idea what would

have happened if she'd tried to save someone's life. Anyway, it was useless even thinking about it now. She was no longer a fixologist.

59. Aeroplane!

Astrid and Kia-Jane had been trying all morning to recharge the phone battery, but all their attempts had failed. Then Kia-Jane had a brainwave. Maybe they could use the power from the solar panels on top of the car to work the phone? She had just climbed out onto the Voovl's roof to check it out, when she suddenly stopped, cocked her head to one side, then peered searchingly up into the wide blue sky.

'Aeroplane!' she yelled.

The Voovl's door popped open and Astrid stuck her head out. 'Where?'

'I can't see it yet,' Kia-Jane said, 'but I can hear it. Listen!'

Astrid heard it straight away – the faint drone of an aircraft. It sounded distant and very high up.

'Quick!' she cried. 'We'll light a signal fire!'

60. Everything you need to know about signal fires

You have probably seen signal fires in movies or read about them in other (less exciting) books. There are two basic types of signal fires: (a) the panic fire; and (b) the sentinel fire/bonfire.

Let's take a look at them in close-up.[55]

(a) The panic fire. The hero/heroine is stranded on an island/in the middle of a desert/in a forest/in the jungle/high in the mountains. She/he has only been there for a few hours/a few days/or perhaps a few weeks if he/she isn't a forward thinker. Suddenly there is the sound of an aeroplane/helicopter/motorboat/bagggoon[56], or a ship appears on the horizon. This throws the heroine/hero into a panic. He/she begins picking up driftwood/collecting dried camel dung/stripping sticks off trees/collecting dried mountain-goat dung and throwing it/them in an untidy (usually damp) pile on the ground. Then she/he spends the next two minutes (if it's a movie) or two pages (if it's a book) trying to light the fire. But it's no use – panic fires don't light. Or if they do, it's always *after* the aeroplane/helicopter/motorboat/bagggoon/ship has disappeared over the horizon, leaving the hero/heroine standing beside their pile of smouldering sticks/camel dung/mountain-goat dung, waving her/his arms in the air and yelling 'He-e-e-ey, he-e-e-ey, he-e-e-ey!' at the top of his/her voice.

Once it finally sinks in that the pilot/driver/bagggoonist/sea-captain hasn't seen or heard him/her, the heroine/hero will sink to his/her knees and spend two minutes/pages sobbing (if they're a polite kind of heroine/hero) or swearing (if they're a not very polite kind of hero/heroine)[57].

---

[55] But not too close – we don't want to get burned.

[56] Well, you never know . . .

[57] But who can blame them? Was that pilot/driver/bagggoonist/sea-captain asleep or something?

After that, the heroine/hero will spend the whole of the next two minutes/pages preparing a huge:

(b) The sentinel fire/bonfire. The heroine/hero is stranded on an island/in the middle of a desert/in a forest/in the jungle/high in the mountains. He/she has been there for a few weeks/a few months, or even a year or more if she/he is Robinson/Rosie Crusoe or Tom/Thomasina Hanks. Suddenly there is the sound of an aeroplane/helicopter/motorboat/bagggoon, or a ship appears on the horizon. This *doesn't* throw the hero/heroine into a panic. She/he makes his/her way in an orderly fashion to a huge pile of dry wood/camel dung/mountain-goat dung, situated on a beach/on a sandhill/in a clearing/on a mountain-top, and calmly sets it alight. Then he/she spends the next two minutes/pages standing beside her/his roaring blaze, waving his/her arms in the air, and yelling, 'He-e-e-ey, he-e-e-ey, he-e-e-ey!' at the top of her/his voice.

Even sentinel fires/bonfires don't always work. In *really* frustrating movies/books the aeroplane/ helicopter/motorboat/bagggoon or ship continues on its way despite the sentinel fire/bonfire *and* five whole minutes/pages of waving and 'He-e-e-ey, he-e-e-ey, he-e-e-ey!'-ing. And as the aeroplane/ helicopter/motorboat/bagggoon or ship disappears over the horizon, the heroine/hero will sink to his/ her knees and spend two minutes/pages sobbing/ swearing.

Anyway, if you've been reading this book carefully, you might be able to guess what type of fire our heroines will light in the next chapter.

61. Bushfire[58]

'Well, derr!' said Kia-Jane. 'How can we light a signal fire? We're on an iceberg!'[59]

'There's a tree[60] on our iceberg,' Astrid pointed out.

'But we are *in* the tree,' Kia-Jane pointed out.[61]

Astrid leaned further out of the car, listening to the drone of the aeroplane, which seemed to be growing louder. 'We'll just burn one branch.' She snapped one off. It was a small dried-up branch with lots of twigs and brown leaves on the end.

'Hold this for a second,' she said, passing the branch up to Kia-Jane.

While she was inside the car getting the

---

58 Ha ha! Tricked you!
59 Old Eskimo saying: People on icebergs should not light fires.
60 Old Eskimo: 'What's a tree?'
61 Old bushman saying: People in trees should not light fires.

matches, Astrid heard Kia-Jane cry out, 'There it is! The aeroplane! I can see it!'

Sure enough, when Astrid stuck her head back out and looked where Kia-Jane was pointing, she saw a tiny dark speck crossing the sky about ten kilometres to the north of them.

'Quick!' she cried, fumbling a match out of the box. 'Hold the branch down here, so I can light it.'

It took Astrid six goes with her clumsy, numb fingers to light a match, but finally the dry leaves on the end of the branch crackled into flame.

'At last!' sighed Kia-Jane, who had eyes only for the aeroplane. She began waving the burning branch back and forth above her head and crying, 'He-e-e-ey, he-e-e-ey, he-e-e-ey!' at the top of her voice.

'He-e-e-ey, he-e-e-ey, he-e-e-ey!' Astrid cried in alarm, but not at the top of *her* voice.

'He-e-e-ey, he-e-e-ey, he-e-e-ey!' went Kia-Jane.

'HE-E-E-EY, HE-E-E-EY, HE-E-E-EY!' cried Astrid, trying to attract Kia-Jane's attention, but still not at the top of her voice.

But Kia-Jane's eyes were glued to the aeroplane. 'He-e-e-ey, he-e-e-ey, he-e-e-ey!' she cried.

'HE-E-E-EY, HE-E-E-EY, HE-E-E-EY!' cried Astrid, still not *quite* at the top of her voice.

'He-e-e-ey, he-e-e-ey, he-e-e-ey!' cried Kia-Jane.

'HE-E-E-EY, HE-E-E-EY, HE-E-E-EY!' cried Astrid, *nearly* at the top of her voice.

'He-e-e-ey, he-e-e-ey, he-e-e-ey!' cried Kia-Jane.

'HE-E-E-EY, HE-E-E-EY, HE-E-E-EY!'

cried Astrid, *finally* at the top of her voice – which was louder than Kia-Jane's, in case you hadn't noticed.

Kia-Jane looked down at her. 'Will you stop doing that, Supe – you'll make me go deaf!'

'Will *you* stop doing *that*!' Astrid said, pointing.

The entire top of the tree above Kia-Jane's head was on fire.[62] [63]

62. Evacuate

'Lukas!' Astrid cried. 'Lukas, wake up!'

His eyes fluttered open. *'Wha's ... wheeze ... going ... wheeze ... on?'*

'The tree's on fire. We have to evacuate.'

With Astrid's help, Lukas managed to sit up and dangle his legs out of the car. Kia-Jane guided his feet onto the rope ladder. Slowly, with Kia-Jane just below him and Astrid just above, the two girls helped Lukas down to the ice. They were just in time. Above them, the whole tree was now a roiling ball of flame. Sparks and cinders fell all around them. Astrid and Kia-Jane carried Lukas over to the edge of the iceberg where a huge crowd of black-and-white penguins (and one pink-and-grey one) stood watching the fire.

'Kraaaaaaak!' said one of them, as the girls lay Lukas carefully on one of the space blankets.

---

62 Old bushman: 'I warned you.'
63 Old Eskimo: 'Will someone please tell me what a tree is?'

'He-e-e-ey, he-e-e-ey, he-e-e-ey!' said another
(the pink-and-grey one), as the girls put the other
space blanket on top of Lukas. Astrid gently smeared
some sunscreen she'd rescued from the emergency
pack on his exposed skin.

'Did you hear that?' asked Kia-Jane. 'One of the
penguins talked.'

'That reminds me,' said Astrid, 'have you seen
the galah lately?'

'Not since Chapter 53.'

Both girls looked up at the Voovl, its paintwork
blistering and turning black in the angry flames.
'Oh, no!' they cried.

'Oh, no!' cried the pink-and-grey penguin.

63. Found

'I'd like to report a bushfire,' said the radio operator
aboard the Air Force Orion as it circled the iceberg.

'Roger,' said a voice in his headset. 'Could you
give me your coordinates so I can notify the
appropriate branch of the Country Fire Authority.'

Roger gave their position. 'Oh, and there's something else,' he added. 'I think we've found those missing kids.'

64. We're saved!

Astrid and Kia-Jane stood beside the flaming tree, waving their arms at the circling aeroplane and yelling, 'He-e-e-ey, he-e-e-ey, he-e-e-ey!' and
'HE-E-E-EY, HE-E-E-EY, HE-E-E-EY!'
at the tops of their voices.

They (well, Astrid) scared the elephant seal and all the penguins, except one, into the sea.

'He-e-e-ey, he-e-e-ey, he-e-e-ey!' yelled the single remaining penguin, waving its pink-and-grey wings at the circling aeroplane.

After about three minutes of circling, the Air Force Orion waggled *its* wings in farewell, then flew away to the north. Which was just as well, because everyone left on the iceberg had just about lost their voice.

'What happens now?' Astrid asked hoarsely.

'I guess they'll send a ship or a helicopter to rescue us,' Kia-Jane said hoarsely.

Astrid hugged herself in relief (and also because she was cold – the tree had burned

nearly all the way down to the ice). 'Our signal fire worked![64] We're saved!'

'We're saved!' Kia-Jane cried hoarsely.

'We're saved!' the pink-and-grey penguin cried hoarsely.

'Kraaaaaaak[65]!' a black-and-white pengin said (hoarsely), as it clambered back onto the iceberg.

Watched by both the penguins, Astrid and Kia-Jane hugged each other and danced in circles on the ice.

65. Help . . . me!

'As . . . trid,' whispered a very faint voice.

Astrid didn't hear it. She and Kia-Jane were standing on the edge of the iceberg searching the northern horizon for aeroplanes, helicopters, motorboats, bagggoons[66] or ships.

'I wonder how long it will take them to get here?' Kia-Jane asked.

'Not too long, I hope,' said Astrid. 'I'm famished!'

Kia-Jane nodded. 'Me, too. Hey, it's a shame we didn't salvage the emergency pack.'

They turned and looked at the Voovl, now a smouldering black hulk in the middle of a puddle of steaming water where the gum tree had stood.

'It was an excellent fire,' Kia-Jane said.

'The best!' said Astrid.

'Shame about the Voovl.'

---

[64] Correction to Chapter 60: Sometimes panic fires do actually work.

[65] 'I live here, plankton-brain!'

[66] Well, you never know.

'Well, it did its job.'

'As . . . trid!'

'No it didn't.' Kia-Jane shook her head. 'It didn't fix the ozone layer.'

'*I* didn't fix the ozone layer,' Astrid corrected her.

'Well, you tried.'

'As . . . trid, I . . . can't . . .'

'I wonder what went wrong? Dr Hu reckoned I was *destroying* the ozone layer.' Astrid looked at her fingers and shivered. 'Now I can't fix anything.'

'. . . breathe!'

'Did you hear that?' Astrid said.

'What?'

'I'm not sure. Listen!'

They both listened.

Suddenly there was a strange creaking, groaning noise.

'Yeah, I heard it that time.'

'Help . . . me!'

'That wasn't what I – '

Astrid's voice was drowned by a loud splintering sound, then the whole iceberg trembled.

'Hey, what's going on?' gasped Kia-Jane.

Beneath their feet, the ice began to buck and tilt and sway. The splintering noise rose in intensity.

'Oh, my gosh!' Astrid cried, pointing. From the centre of the iceberg, where the burnt-out Voovl sat, a series of spider-web cracks radiated out across the ice in all directions. 'The iceberg's falling apart!'[67]

---

[67] Old Eskimo: 'Next time they'll take more notice of old Eskimo sayings.'

66. A very bad dream

'Look out!' yelled Kia-Jane, as a huge crack shot straight towards them, growing wider as it came. She leapt out of the way. So did a couple of penguins. Astrid was about to follow when she remembered Lukas. Grabbing the bottom space blanket, she slid him out of the crack's path with only a second to spare. The crack reached the edge of the iceberg and – CRUNCH! – the whole iceberg split in two.

'Phew! That was too close for comfort,' Astrid gasped, as they and the penguins teetered on the edge of the half-iceberg.

But it wasn't over yet.

'Incoming crack at four o'clock!' yelled Kia-Jane.

This time they both slid Lukas out of the way.

CRUNCH! Now they were on a piece of iceberg shaped like a quarter of a pizza (without anchovies).

'Here comes another one!'

CRUNCH!

Now they were on a wedge of iceberg shaped like an eighth of a pizza.

'And again!' cried Kia-Jane.

CRUNCH!

This time they had jumped in opposite directions. Kia-Jane balanced on one-sixteenth of an iceberg pizza, Astrid and Lukas on another. Several penguins, including the pink-and-grey one, stood on another wedge 30 metres away. The girls looked nervously in the direction of the Voovl. There was a sudden bubbling noise, a cloud of steam, then the burnt-out car wreck disappeared slowly into the ocean. They held their breaths, waiting for more cracks to appear, but none did.

'What do we do now?' Astrid called across the three-metre gap separating their mini-icebergs.

'It's too far to jump,' said Kia-Jane. 'Let's just hope we don't drift too far apart. How's Lukas?'

Astrid sat down next to him. His eyes were closed. 'Lukas, you'll never guess what just happen– Lukas? Lukas? *Lukas!*'

'What's wrong?'

'He isn't breathing!'

Kia-Jane laughed nervously. 'Of course he's breathing! You shouldn't make jokes about it, Supe.'

'I'm *not* joking, Kia-Jane,' cried Astrid, her eyes welling with tears. 'He *isn't* breathing.'

'Well . . . do something . . .' Kia-Jane came to the very edge of her iceberg.

'*What?*' Astrid asked her.

Kia-Jane was silent for a few seconds. She was biting her lower lip. 'Listen!' she said.

In the distance, very faintly, Astrid heard the most welcome sound that had ever reached her ears.

'A helicopter!'

'They'll have a puffer,' Kia-Jane said, sounding relieved. 'Lukas's parents will have told them he's got asthma.'

Astrid stood up. The little pizza-slice-shaped iceberg wobbled slightly beneath her shifting weight. She shielded her eyes against the glare of the sun. There it was – a tiny black dot hung just above the horizon. It was heading straight towards them.

'Do you think they'll have a doctor aboard?' Astrid asked.

'They're sure to,' said Kia-Jane.

Astrid watched the helicopter approach. It was so slow. Too slow. Everything seemed to be happening in slow motion. It felt like a dream, a very bad dream. Lukas wasn't breathing.

He was not breathing!

Suddenly Astrid knew what she had to do.

Kneeling on the ice, she bent down over Lukas, tipped his head back and put her mouth to his.

67. Kiss of life

Astrid had learned mouth-to-mouth resuscitation
at her swimming club. They used a dummy called
Fred. Fred didn't look like a real person. He had
a smooth round head and a mouth that tasted
like plastic.

Lukas wasn't like Fred. Up close, his skin had
freckles and at least four pimples (though Astrid
wasn't counting), and there were lots of tiny dark
hairs above his upper lip. And his mouth tasted
like ... well, a *mouth*. Worse, his crooked teeth and
Astrid's nice straight ones bumped together. Closing
her eyes, Astrid pretended it was Fred and blew a
big breath into Lukas's lungs. Then she turned her
head to one side like she'd been taught, gasped some
more air, and did it again.

Please start breathing! she thought. *Please please,
Lukas, get better!*

Halfway through the fourth breath, Astrid
sensed a change. She opened her eyes. From two
centimetres away, a big eye was staring straight back
at her. It wasn't Fred's. And her tongue seemed to
have a life of its own – it was poking around against
her teeth and tickling the inside of her lips. *Hang
on*, Astrid thought, *that isn't* my *tongue!* (It wasn't
Fred's either.)

'Yick!' she cried, and sprang back so quickly she
nearly rolled off the iceberg.

Lukas coughed a couple of times, then slowly

stood up. His face was bright red. 'Um, thanks, Astrid,' he said.

'Don't mention it,' Astrid stammered, lying on the ice and rubbing her mouth with the back of her hand. Her face was just as red as Lukas's.[68] 'Are you okay now?'

'I'm fine,' he said, shyly offering her his hand. 'Actually, I feel better than I have for years.'

Astrid shyly accepted it and was helped to her feet. 'Thanks, Lukas,' she said, avoiding his eyes.

'You're welcome, Astrid,' he said, avoiding hers.

Kia-Jane, on the next iceberg over, wasn't avoiding anyone's eyes. She was pretending to hold a pair of binoculars. 'I spy with my little eye, a pair of lovebirds!'

'Kia-Jane,' Astrid and Lukas both said together, 'take a jump!'

68. %#*@<&!!!

Kia-Jane didn't realise how good Astrid's and Lukas's advice to take a jump was until she looked behind her. A huge elephant seal was clambering onto her iceberg.

'Shoo!' she cried. She flapped her hands at it. 'Shoo! Shoo! Shoo!'

Elephant seals are huge. They aren't really bothered when someone tells them to 'shoo' (though 'HE-E-E-EY, HE-E-E-EY, HE-E-E-EY!' works quite well). This one kept coming. Its massive

[68] Or a red rose.

weight tilted the iceberg to an alarming angle. Kia-Jane looked imploringly at the sky, but the helicopter was still half a kilometre away.

'Take a jump!' yelled a strangely familiar voice that came from the middle of a crowd of penguins on a nearby iceberg.

Kia-Jane didn't need any further encouragement. Bending her knees, she tensed like a spring, then leapt across the three-metre gap separating her iceberg from the one Astrid and Lukas were on.

It was a good jump. Unfortunately, the landing was not quite so good. As soon as Kia-Jane's feet hit the ice, they shot out from under her. She landed on her backside, with a loud crunch that rocked the whole iceberg.

'Ouch!' Lukas said sympathetically.

Remember Chapter 60? Remember how there are two kinds of hero/heroine – polite ones and not very polite ones? Well, it seems that Kia-Jane was the not very polite kind of heroine.

What she said when her backside made contact with the ice can't be printed in a children's book. Worse, she said it so loudly that the elephant seal on the next iceberg over (which hadn't been at all bothered by Kia-Jane's 'Shoo! Shoo! Shoo!') slid back into the water with a shocked expression on its face.

Astrid helped Kia-Jane to her feet. 'Are you okay?'

'No,' she wailed, grimacing and bending forward like a little old lady (or like a little young one who had just had a very painful accident). 'I think I've broken my bum!'[69]

69. A not very polite galah

The helicopter arrived and lowered a paramedic with a stretcher. The stretcher was for Lukas but he no longer needed it – Kia-Jane did. The paramedic strapped her in securely, then she and the paramedic were winched up into the helicopter. Lukas and Astrid climbed a rope ladder.

Just before the helicopter's door closed, there was a flurry of wings and a pink-and-grey shape came hurtling in. It landed on Astrid's shoulder.

'Why, hullo!' Astrid said. 'We thought we'd lost you in the bushfire.'

'%#*@<&!!!'[70] replied the galah, bobbing its head up and down and giving her an affectionate nip on the ear.

[69] A polite heroine would probably say, 'I think I have sustained a rather embarrassing injury.'

[70] The galah wasn't a polite hero/heroine, either.

'Ouch!'

Dr Hu was in the helicopter. He hugged Lukas, then he hugged Astrid and Kia-Jane, as well.

'Ouch!' said Kia-Jane.

She couldn't sit down. She had to stand up, holding on to a ceiling strap, all the way to the rescue ship. It took 20 minutes, and along the way they told Dr Hu everything that had happened.

Then Dr Hu explained how, after hearing they were on an iceberg, Astrid's mother had raced up to her observatory on Mount Stringybark and used a satellite-mounted telescope to search the Antarctic Ocean from up in space. It didn't take her long to find their iceberg – it was the only one with a gum tree on it, after all.

'I was already on the rescue ship when she phoned,' Dr Hu explained. 'The Navy sent an aeroplane out at first light and they saw your signal fire.'

'It wasn't really a signal fire,' Astrid admitted. 'We didn't mean to burn the Voovl.'

Dr Hu smiled. 'The main thing is, you three are safe.'

'Kraaaaaaak!' said the galah.

'Sorry,' Dr Hu apologised. 'You *four!*'

70. It's up to all of us

'There's something I don't understand,' Astrid said. 'Why couldn't I fix the ozone layer?'

Dr Hu shook his head. 'It's my fault. I should have realised what was going to happen.'

'What *did* happen?'

'It's quite simple, really,' he said. 'You see, ozone (O_3) is an allotrope of oxygen, made up of three oxygen atoms. It's formed when the more stable oxygen molecule (O_2) is split by ultravoilet radiation and – '

'Da-a-a-a-ad!' Lukas interrupted him. 'That's *not* simple! We're kids, not scientists.'

'Sorry,' he said. 'Let me put it another way. Since ozone is formed when oxygen is broken down, Astrid *couldn't* fix it. All she could fix was the oxygen.'

Astrid frowned. 'So instead of turning oxygen into ozone, I turned ozone into oxygen?'

'Precisely,' said Dr Hu. 'Luckily, the ozone at the edge of the hole is very thinly distributed, so you didn't start a chain reaction. Not much damage was done.'

'But what will happen to the ozone layer?' asked Kia-Jane.

Dr Hu spread his hands. 'It's up to *all* of us now. If we stop polluting the air, the ozone layer might well repair itself over the next 50 years or so.'

71. Kia-Jane's bottom[71]

Kia-Jane's bottom was a bit like the ozone layer – it would repair itself. Only it wouldn't take 50 years.

[71] Not to be confused with Mrs Hudson's bottom (see footnote 34) which was somewhat larger, and had echidna spines poking out of it. (For more details, see *Echidna Mania*, available at a bookshop near you.)

'In six weeks you should be able to sit down again,' the ship's doctor informed her.

This wasn't good news to Kia-Jane. 'Six *weeks*?'

She was standing in the doctor's surgery aboard the rescue ship, *Burke and Wills*, with her jeans around her ankles. Fortunately for Kia-Jane (who, although not always a very polite kind of heroine, was a modest one) the doctor was a woman.

'You've broken your tail-bone,' the doctor explained. 'That's the bone at the base of your spine. There's nothing to be done for an injury of this kind, I'm afraid. All I can suggest is you ask your parents to buy you a really comfortable pair of shoes.'

72. Aaaah!

Lukas was next to be examined. The doctor took a long time listening to his chest.

'Are you sure you have asthma?' she asked.

Lukas nodded.

'He's had it all his life,' said Dr Hu, who had accompanied his son into the ship's surgery.

The other doctor was looking puzzled. 'And you say you had a bad attack while you were on the iceberg?'

'I passed right out,' said Lukas. '*And* I stopped breathing. Astrid had to give me the kiss of . . . I mean, mouth-to-mouth resuscitation,' he corrected himself, turning pink as a galah (or a pink rose).

'Hmmm,' said the doctor, listening to his heart now. 'Well, I must say I can detect no after-effects.'

She stuck a tongue depressor into his mouth. 'Say *aaaah*.'

'*Aaaah!*' said Lukas.

The doctor straightened up and smiled. 'Well, if you *were* unconscious, you have made a wonderful recovery. You seem to be in perfect health, young man.'

Lukas frowned, and said '*Aaaah!*' again.

Both doctors looked at him, puzzled.

'*Aaaah! Aaaah! Aaaah!*'

'Lukas,' his father said, 'I don't think you have to do that any more.'

'Dad, listen. *Aaaah!* I don't squeak and rasp any more!'

'Hmmmm,' said his father, frowning more than ever. 'Would you open your mouth again, please, Lukas.'

He opened his mouth.

'Lukas, what has happened to your teeth?' Dr Hu asked.

73. Still a fixologist!

'Astrid! Astrid!' Lukas called, as he came racing up the steps to the bridge of the *Burke and Wills*. 'Guess what?'

The ship's captain had been giving the girls and the galah (it was perched happily on the Captain's shoulder like a pirate's parrot) a tour of the ship. Kia-Jane was at the helm.

'Here comes your boyfriend, Supe.'

'Shut up, Kia-Jane.'

Lukas came flying in the door. 'Astrid! You're still a fixologist!'

'What are you talking about?' she asked.

'You know how your fingers don't work any more?' he said excitedly. 'Well, your lips do.'

'My *lips*?' Astrid said.

'Yeah, your lips.' Lukas turned to the Captain. 'Sir, may I borrow your pencil?'

The Captain gave him a pencil. Lukas promptly snapped it in half.

'Hey!' said the Captain.

'He-e-e-ey! He-e-e-ey! He-e-e-ey!' said the galah.

'It's okay,' Lukas told them. He held both pieces up towards Astrid's face. 'Kiss it.'

'Kiss it?' she said.

'Kiss it.'

'You want me to kiss it?'

'That's right.'

'You want me to *kiss* the pencil?'

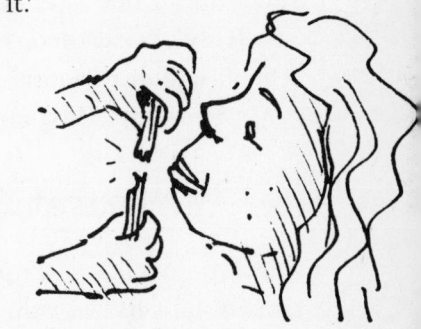

The galah rolled its eyes. 'Just kiss the pencil, Astrid.'

She shrugged. 'Okay,' she said, and, wishing Lukas hadn't broken it in the first place, Astrid kissed the pencil.

'Tah daa!' said Lukas, holding it up.

It was fixed!

'That's unbelievable,' said the Captain.

'I told you!' Lukas beamed at Astrid. 'You're still a fixologist. Only now you fix things with your lips, not your fingers.'

Astrid gripped the bench in front of her. It was taking a few moments for this to sink in. She was still a fixologist! She could fix things by *kissing* them!

'Lukas, how did you work it out?'

He opened his mouth.

'Did I do *that*?' asked Astrid, amazed.

'Yes, you fixed my teeth,' Lukas said handsomely. 'You fixed my voice, as well,' he said smoothly. 'And my asthma,' he said healthily. 'Astrid,' he said lovingly, 'I could kiss – 72'

They never found out what Lukas could kiss, because at that very moment the ship lurched suddenly to one side and everyone nearly fell over.

'Hey!' cried the Captain, making a grab for the wheel, which Kia-Jane had suddenly let go.

'He-e-e-ey! He-e-e-ey! He-e-e-ey!' cried the galah.

74. Secret girls' business

'Kia-Jane, what's the matter?' Astrid asked as soon as the Captain had steadied the ship.

'Come with me.' Kia-Jane beckoned for Astrid to accompany her outside. 'Not you, Lukas,' she said, when he started following them, too. 'This is girls' stuff.'

72 Myself? The pencil? The galah?

'What is it?' Astrid asked, as soon as they were alone.

Kia-Jane seemed hesitant. Which was unusual. Kia-Jane was *never* hesitant. 'Astrid,' she said shyly, 'you know how we've been best friends ever since we started school?'

'Yes,' said Astrid.

'And you know how best friends do favours for each other?'

'Yes,' said Astrid.

'And how sometimes they even do each other really *special* favours?'

'Yes,' said Astrid.

'Well, Astrid Spark, my very bestest friend in the whole wide world, I've got a really really really *HUGE* favour to ask of you.'

'Yes?' said Astrid.

Kia-Jane's face turned red.[73] 'You know how I can't sit down for six weeks?'

'Yes,' said Astrid.

'This is really embarrassing . . .'

'Yes?' said Astrid.

'Well . . . ,' Kia-Jane murmured.

'Yes?' said Astrid.

'Just say it, Kia-Jane!' shrieked a passing seagull.

Kia-Jane pointed at the region of her recent injury. 'Astrid, will you please please please please *please* kiss my butt?'

---

[73] As a you-know-what.

75. Meanwhile, back in Tasmania . . .

A Country Fire Authority fire truck pulled up on a beach right down at the southernmost tip of the island state. The driver switched off the siren and eight puzzled firemen climbed out.

'They *did* say a forest fire?' asked the fire-chief, peering out to sea.

'They definitely said a forest fire,' said his second-in-command, also peering out to sea.

'*South* of here?' asked the fire-chief.

'South of here,' said his second-in-command.

With a puzzled frown, the fire-chief surveyed the deserted windswept beach in both directions. 'Okay, men,' he said finally, 'I suppose we had better establish a firebreak.'

76. Meanwhile, up in space . . .

'Vladimir,' Colonel Randy said irritably, 'look what that animal has done!'

The Daily Inter-Planet had arrived by spacefax only fifteen minutes ago, but already it was soggy and chewed.

Major Vladimir smiled with pride. 'Isn't she a most clever cosmodog! Next I will be teaching her for to fetch your new slippers.'

'Please don't bother,' Colonel Randy said grumpily, shaking Marie Curie drool off the remains of the newspaper. 'How am I supposed to read this?'

'Don't be getting in a knot your under-garments, Baby Randy,' Major Vladimir advised him. 'As they are in your country saying, good news is no news.'

'But I wanted to read about those children who went missing in that balloon,' said Colonel Randy. He gingerly opened the tattered newspaper. 'Ah, here it is. Look – they've been found!'

'Over the moon!' cried Major Vladimir, clasping Marie Curie's front paws and doing a nimble foxtrot with her up one wall, across the ceiling and down the other side. 'A happy ending I am loving, one hundred per cent!'

77. Another happy ending

Kia-Jane sat on the ship's rail waving to the people down on the wharf. 'There's a big crowd.'

'Of course there is,' said Lukas. 'We're front page news. Everyone knows what happened.'

'Thank goodness they don't know *everything* that happened,' murmured Astrid, whose lips had been scrubbed red-raw and still tasted a bit soapy.

'Kiss my butt!' whispered the galah.

'In your dreams,' Astrid whispered back.

'I can see your parents, Supe.' Kia-Jane pointed. 'See? They're talking to that guy with the microphone.'

Astrid groaned. 'Why are all those reporters here?'

'Because we're heroes.'

'We're not heroes. All we did was get lost and have to be rescued. I couldn't even fix the ozone layer.'

'You saved my life,' Lukas said.

'You saved my bu– [74]' Kia-Jane began, but Dr Hu arrived at that moment, interrupting her.

'Come on, you three, they're waiting for us down on the wh– [75]'

'Ahem!' coughed the galah.

'Come on, you *four*, they're waiting for us down on the whomblebomble.'

'*Whomblebomble?*' chorused all of them except the galah.

'*Whomblebomble?*' chorused the galah (late as usual).

Dr Hu's face turned red.[76] 'Embarrassing! I don't know where that came from. I meant the wharf. We have to give a press conference on the *wharf*.'

'Press conference!!!?' Astrid shook her head. 'Sorry, Dr Hu, but I'm not allowed to talk to the press.'

---

[74] Budgerigar? Burger? Bunny rabbit?

[75] Whaler? Whirligig? Whomblebomble?

[76] As a rose. (A *red* one, not a pink one, a yellow one, a white one, or one of those orange-and-red stripey ones.)

She was wrong. This time she *was* allowed to talk to the press. In fact, Dr Hu insisted on it. So did her parents.

Astrid was wrong about not being a hero, too. She *was* a hero. All three of them . . . ('Ahem!') Sorry . . . all *four* of them were heroes. Because even though they hadn't been able to repair the ozone layer, their attempt drew worldwide attention to the problem. Lots of countries reduced the manufacture of ozone-destroying chemicals, and people everywhere became more aware of the dangers of pollution and the benefits of recycling.

And the sale of sunscreen and hats went through the roof. Ms Chapeau held a garage sale and took a world cruise on the proceeds.

'The ozone layer is far from fixed,' Dr Hu said at a special dinner held in the bagggoonists' honour that Christmas. 'But thanks to these brave young people . . .'

'Ahem!'

'. . . and galah, the whole world is united in an effort to save it.'

And that's the end, really. Everyone lives happily ever after.

Well, not everyone, obviously, but everyone in this book. Especially Lukas, who becomes Astrid's boyfriend and goes on to become the healthiest person in the world. And Astrid herself, who becomes a politician, and then Australia's first female prime minister, because when she kisses babies ... she gets their parents' votes every time.

The End

'Ahem!'

The galah? Last I heard, it was dating a penguin and looking for somewhere to settle down and hatch some eggs – ideally a nice stable iceberg with a gum tree on it, close to a school[77] if possible. If you know of one either for sale or for rent, please let me know and I'll pass the information on.

[77] Of fish.